NIGHTMARE DETECTIVE
~THE SKELETON KING~

MONK INYANG

Nightmare Detective: The Skeleton King

Nightmare Detective: The Skeleton King

Monk Inyang

Illustrated by
Elijah Isaiah Johnson

SUNTEXT PUBLISHING / NEWARK

Suntext Publishing

146B Ferry St. B-1

Suite #1069

Newark, NJ 07105

www.monkinyang.com

Publisher's Note: This is a work of fiction. Names, characters, places, and incidents are a product of the author's imagination. Locales and public names are sometimes used for atmospheric purposes. Any resemblance to actual people, living or dead, or to businesses, companies, events, institutions, or locales is completely coincidental.

Book design © 2018 BookDesignTemplates.com

Ordering Information: Special discounts are available on quantity purchases by corporations, associations, and others. For details, contact the publisher at the address above.

Newark / Monk Inyang — First Edition

ISBN 978-1-7325432-0-1

Printed in the United States of America

For Amah, Rose, & Elijah.
To the village who helped grow the seed
and to Chelsie, for her nightmare.

Contents

CHAPTER 1

Haunted Houseguests

UKO HILL'S HEAD SHOT UP after a boom so loud it woke him from his peaceful sleep. He squinted as he scanned his pitch-black room but could not see the cause of the disturbance. As a twelve-year-old boy in a busy house, he was used to the random nighttime noises that turned out to be harmless. He was sure this was the same.

Just as he relaxed enough to lay his head back down, a second crash rattled him. He was now certain it was a heavy knock on the front door downstairs. As he wondered what could be so urgent in the middle of the night, a loud voice called out his name.

"Oooo - kooohhhh"

The voice was a raspy growl that could not be of this world. The bass of each syllable overwhelmed the room's silence and echoed in Uko's chest.

The knock repeated, somehow louder, somehow more threatening. The voice recast its grisly call. Uko's eyes widened and his ears perked up as he tried to determine if all of this was real. He looked longingly towards his pillow in hopes that it would tell him that he was just hearing things. Against his better judgement, Uko placed his feet on the ground and stood up. He immediately noticed the cold dampness of the carpet against his bare feet. He looked down to see what he may have stepped in, but the room was still too dark to tell. He slowly walked into the hallway of the small house. "How can everyone else sleep through this?" he wondered aloud as he looked over the hall's banister. With the help of the moonlight streaming in the large windows of the foyer, he could see the home's front door rattle with each knock. His face dropped at the sight. This had to be real.

Uko slinked down the stairs toward the door, each step damper than the last. The awkward feeling of wet carpet sent chills through his body as he crept. Midway down he could hear the slosh of his feet in a jet-black puddle beneath him. At the bottom of the stairs, he paused. His brain screamed at him to turn around and run back upstairs, but every muscle in his body fought that urge, and he inched forward. He felt as if an invisible force was pulling him to the door. *Why is this happening to me?* He thought as he shakily took each step.

The knocking stopped and the voice whispered to him, "Almost there, fine boy. Open the door please."

Uko waded through the flooded foyer toward the door. As he placed his trembling hand on the door's cold handle, it crashed opened with the furious violence of something exploding. The light from outside blinded him. He squinted. An unfamiliar silhouette took shape in front of him. Twenty, perhaps fifty, hooded figures, stood around the small entrance to his family's home. The figures looked skeletal. His jaw dropped with the figure directly in front of him. The inside of the creature's eye sockets cracked, and exposed fiery balls of piercing light that looked like small suns dancing inside its head. The hooded figure returned Uko's stare by placing its palm on his shoulder.

It was only the complete cold of the palm, a cold so intense that it burned, that forced Uko to move from his frozen state and look at the hand. It was made of bone and nothing more as it rested its weight on Uko. The figure's shadowy face and glowing eyes broke into a lipless smile. With that, Uko felt blood rush back into hands and feet. He screamed, turned, and ran. He charged up the riverbed steps toward his family: his mother, his father, his older brother. If there was ever a moment he needed them, this was it.

"Everyone, wake up! Help!" he pleaded with all of his might despite the lack of air in his lungs. He bounded up the stairs three at a time while splashing water soaked his pants. At the top he briefly turned. The skeletal figures poured in through the open front door. The skeleton whose voice compelled Uko and whose palm burned his shoulder, held its place at the entrance - the smile still across its face.

Uko burst into his parent's room and raced to their bed. He tried to shake them from their sleep as the evil figures closed in.

"Mommy! Daddy, wake up. Wake up! Wake up!"

He shook and shook his parents, but they never woke. Uko's eyes welled with tears.

"Please, I need you! They're coming. Come on, wake up!"

Despite every effort to rock them from their slumber, they did not respond. Meanwhile, the house was washed in sound as the figures raided every room but the one Uko currently occupied. He crawled to the room's closet and closed the door. He crouched as low as he could against the back wall and threw clothes on top of himself for good measure. He pulled his knees up to his chin and tried to calm the trembling in his body by rocking back and forth.

The din of noise fell silent as he waited. In that silence he realized what was happening. This was all a repeat of horrors he had already witnessed.

He had been through this before and he knew how it ended.

"My fine boy, Uko, why are you hiding from me?" the familiar voice drawled.

This time it didn't echo from behind a door outside. It floated to him from within the room. Uko's rocking immediately stopped and his head shot up in the direction of the voice outside the closet. He bit his lip as a last-ditch attempt to keep from screaming.

"I only want to meet you. Talk to you. Shake your hand," the voice said calmly. Uko heard pleasure in the growl, as if he was being taunted.

The voice grew closer with each sentence. With the final words it was at its clearest, delivered by something that must be standing directly outside his closet refuge. Uko took a very deep breath and held it while he prepared for what he knew came next. The closet doors broke open and that same skeletal figure stood before him smiling. It stared into Uko's eyes and breathed in his fear.

"Boo!"

***

Uko screamed as he bolted up from bed, his heart throbbing through his chest.

"Coco. Coco, are you ok?" Uko's mother called out from downstairs. "It's time for breakfast."

"Yes, I'm fine." He scanned his room and pinched his forearm to make sure this was really happening this time. "I'm coming down!"

He was in his little bedroom. It was bright. The floor was dry. His most important possession, a stuffed lion named Kanju, sat on his dresser and stared back at him in silence. Ever since his mom bought him as a souvenir from her trip to Mali, Kanju had been the quiet bodyguard who watched over Uko at night, and welcomed him to the day when he awoke. Uko would rather swallow a live frog than tell anyone about his stuffed animal and hear them forever laugh at his childishness. His mom always told Uko there was nothing wrong with keeping Kanju for so long, but she was biased. She's supposed to say stuff like that.

Uko's mom, dad, and his older brother Femi watched him with concern as he descended the stairs to join them at the kitchen table.

"Are you alright, Cocoa Bean? Was it the same bad dream?" his mom asked.

She's called him Coco ever since he was a baby "with a cocoa bean shaped head" as she liked to lovingly say. She reserved the full nickname, Cocoa Bean, for moments when she was most worried about him.

"The same one every time, Mommy," Uko replied. He may be twelve and on his way to middle school in the fall, but he said Mommy and Daddy like every other Nigerian kid he knew.

"The question is, did you get Mommy and Daddy to wake up this time or nah?" his older brother Femi joked. Their dad shot him a glaring look. "What? I'm kidding."

"Coco, I don't want you watching scary movies before bed. In fact, I think you boys shouldn't watch any of those crazy shows when it's getting close to bedtime. You have overactive imaginations and your minds are running a mile-a-minute when you should be falling asleep." Every week Uko's mom had a new strategy to combat the recurring nightmares.

Femi ruffled Uko's hair and added, "We just need to get you to spend more time around people. Build up your self-confidence and you won't worry about monsters getting you in the middle of the night. You're too uptight, buddy. What if you came with me to the skating rink today? There's gonna be a bunch of kids there."

"No thanks. I'm meeting up with Manny and we're going to Branch Brook to check in on the turtles."

Ever since his family moved from a small apartment in Chicago to their house in Newark, New Jersey, Uko had been most at home at Branch Brook Park. Since he and his best friend Manny were curious five-year-olds, they'd attempted to explore every nook and cranny of the massive land. They overturned every mossy rock, climbed every wrinkled tree, ran through every dewy field, and learned every secret shortcut. Manny was always the strong and more adventurous one during their park missions, but Uko held up when he had to. Each summer, they appointed themselves deputy Park Rangers and spent their days roaming the park grounds. This summer, they found a family of turtles near a pond on the far end of the park. Now their days mainly consisted of hanging out with the turtles while playing video games on their phones. Today was particularly important since Uko and Manny set it aside to name those turtles. They figured if people named their pets, they shouldn't feel weird about naming the park's turtles.

"It's the first day of summer break and you want to skip the skating rink to visit some turtles? Is that right?"

"Yes, Femi. We're naming them today. We're having a ceremony."

"That sounds fun, Coco. If you and Manny decide to name one after me, I won't be opposed to it," Uko's dad said as he laughed at his own joke. He looked around with an exaggerated smile to see if anyone else found the joke as funny as he did. No one smiled back.

"We have an extensive list. But we're voting on each one, so I'll bring it up and see what happens. Thanks for breakfast, I'm gonna grab some snacks for the ceremony and meet Manny outside," Uko said.

"Oooo-kooohhh! Oooo-kooohhh!" a voice yelled from outside their house.

Uko stuck his head outside his living room window to respond to his best friend calling him.

"I can hear you loud and clear, Manny," Uko called out. "I'm coming down."

Manny was a short and muscular boy with dark, curly hair and thick, bushy eyebrows. He met Uko when Manny's family moved in next door right after his fifth birthday. For Manny's parents, it was an opportunity to move out of their small apartment in New York and into a house of their own on a quiet street near a park. For Manny, it was the introduction to his future best friend and partner in crime.

Ever since they met, Manny and Uko were inseparable. Manny loved going to Uko's house for "Hill Family Game Night" and Uko loved going to Manny's house for dinner and his mom's world famous pernil and mofongo. For each of them, the other boy was their brother who lived next door.

"I've come up with some ideas for the turtle naming ceremony. We want as big a crowd as possible, so we need to bring everyone out" Manny said as he and Uko crossed the street from their homes and into the park. They discussed the logistics as they squeezed between kids playing chase and dogs playing fetch.

"You're right, it's a big day for those little guys," Uko said.

"I brought some candy, so we can put that down to bring the ants out. I have my jar with the lightning bugs. It won't be dark during the ceremony, so we won't be able to see them too well but that's fine. I also have a spare bag of peanuts for the squirrels," Manny reported.

"The squirrels are too unpredictable. They're all over the place. Plus, as soon as we run out of peanuts they leave. I have two pieces of toast from breakfast. I'm gonna make a breadcrumb trail from the pond. We should be able to get a whole family of ducks. It'll be a good turnout," Uko replied. They lowered their voices as they walked deeper into the park, or "The Jungle" as they called it, where the tightly packed trees blocked the sunlight. Things were quieter, and you could disappear in peace.

They walked through The Jungle to the pond where they first saw the turtles. The smell of the wet grass, the calmness of the water, and the sounds of the ducks as they jumped in were comforting. Uko and Manny felt at home there. The ants, spiders, squirrels, worms, and turtles were the best kinds of friends to have. They didn't gossip like some kids at school, they never hurt your feelings, and they were always happy to share a meal with you. Sometimes Femi made fun of Uko and Manny for spending so much time with animals instead of people, but this is what they preferred. Maybe one day they would both grow up to be zookeepers and hang out with animals all day. For now, they would have to settle for being Park Rangers of The Jungle.

In the back of Uko's mind he could hear a small voice reminding him that at some point he would have to get back to bed. Sooner or later it would be nighttime, and he would be alone. He'd eventually fall asleep and that same nightmare would haunt him like it had consistently for the last two weeks.

CHAPTER 2

Secret Society

THAT NIGHT UKO LAID AWAKE in his bed doing his best to stay up as long as he could. He had already finished rereading all his favorite comics and listened to Femi's endless story about his day at the skating rink. Multiple times during the boring story he thought about telling Femi that he'd had enough, but Uko was too nice to say so. Now he stared at the ceiling exhausted with no other options to delay the inevitable. Before drifting off, he tried his newest tactic of going through his happiest thoughts. He thought about the park and the turtles. He imagined him and Manny mustering up enough courage to go skating with Femi next time. He imagined that Femi would introduce them to the DJ who would play any song they requested for the entire day. Then they would stroll back through the park on their way home and laugh about the great time on the ice. They'd play video games at Manny's house, have dinner, and then go to bed.

After that version of events, Uko imagined at least twenty more. Each time he had on the dopest clothes, told the funniest jokes, and had the wittiest responses to everything. He was always clever enough to think of the perfect thing to say or do in any situation. As long as he was imagining it, there wasn't anything that could stump him; the problem was doing it in real life.

After version 24 of a perfect day, Uko smiled and peacefully fell asleep as happy as he could be.

***

Almost immediately he was awakened by the sound of someone kicking down the front door of his family's home. He looked around confused. The intense banging ripped through the house again, causing a ringing in his ears.

"Mom! Dad! Someone's knocking on the door," he yelled out from bed. No one answered. Instead, the knock at the door repeated itself. Uko sat up and placed his feet on the ground as he stood. The carpet was cold and noticeably wet. He stared down at his feet with a weird feeling of déjà vu. "Why is that so familiar?" he said aloud as he squished the carpet between his toes. He looked around at his room, his mind racing as it tried to figure out why he felt like this had happened before. He slid out of his room and looked over the hall's banister toward the rattling front door.

He called down with a question he hoped would go unanswered. "Who is it?" he said.

Instead he heard the reply of a familiar growl.

"Oooo - kooohhh. It's me, old friend. Open the door."

Uko's heart began beating loud enough for him to hear over the knocking at the door. Uko was now well aware of what was going on. That familiar voice made it all too clear. Some nights he glided through these nightmares oblivious until deep into the ordeal. But there were nights like tonight when he knew immediately what was happening. He was back in the terrible nightmare that engulfed every sleeping hour. He would try to do things differently on these nights of self-awareness, but the results were always the same. The imposing lead Reaper he named The Skeleton King would barge into his house, find Uko, and kill him. Sometimes he would use an old, gnarled blade. Sometimes The Skeleton King would use his own cold hand. Other times one of his fifty or so henchmen would do the deed.

Either way it always ended with Uko's demise and his unpleasant jolt back to reality.

"N-n-no," Uko replied while summoning what little courage he had. It took all his effort to speak, yet he was still only able to whimper the word.

"What did you say, boy?" The Skeleton King bellowed with anger and astonishment coating his words.

Uko gulped hard before replying with a little more volume, "I said, no." He immediately scrambled down the hallway from his room toward Femi's bedroom. He decided that tonight was as good as any to go down fighting. In his many attempts to beat The Skeleton King and his Reapers, Uko always ran to his parents for assistance. He was so used to them protecting him from everything in his everyday life that his mind always came to them first in his nightmare moment of crisis. Tonight, he decided to change his tactic. He burst into his brother's room with the sole intention of recruiting him for what came next. They would fight the Reaper army together somehow and save their family from annihilation.

Uko shook Femi in his bed with all his might.

"Femi, wake up. He's here. We have to fight. Wake up!"

The jolting did nothing to Femi's limp body. Like Uko's parents countless times before, his brother did not respond. He turned Femi onto his back and looked at a face stiffened by deep slumber and pleaded for help.

"Femi, please! What's wrong with you?"

The only response Uko heard was the crashing open of the home's front door and the ghastly stomping of the Reaper army storming in. Uko could hear The Skeleton King yell to him from the foyer below.

"There is no one here but us, boy!"

Uko returned to shaking his brother with a half-hearted effort. But, Femi would not wake up and save him from this doom. There was no hope in trying. The Skeleton King was correct. It was only him and Uko. It always was and always would be. As the realization sunk in, Uko pulled himself from the bed and fought his tears on the way to the closet. He curled into the farthest corner and closed the door behind him. He sat cross legged in the cold puddle of water in his tiny prison and stared ahead. Even though the noise of destruction was deafening around him, Uko sighed a deep breath and sat motionless. His blank stare settled on the door knob in front of him. For yet another night, he gave up on the belief that he could save himself or his family. As hope drained from his spirit, color drained from his vision until his surroundings turned to shades of gray. Uko listened as the evil army ran through the house breaking mirrors and tearing up furniture. They squealed high pitched laughs of glee as they tore holes in the walls. He looked at the gray clothes around him, his gray arms and legs, and the gray carpet below him while he waited for the end to come. He didn't have the energy to scream or cry, he just stared ahead in exhausted defeat.

After a few moments, an odd sensation overcame Uko. The same way a stranger's gaze can somehow be felt against your skin, Uko could sense that he was suddenly not alone. He turned to what was previously an empty space to his left. Instead of seeing the colorless pile of clothes that greeted him when he first entered, Uko saw the bright smile of a girl looking back at him. She had chestnut brown skin and large almond colored eyes that contrasted with her ash colored surroundings. She sat with a full and perfectly curly afro that draped over her shoulders. Her bright red t-shirt and shining gold bracelet were the last things that Uko expected to see in that moment.

She smiled with a warmth and confidence that did not suit the closet they were huddled in. "Do not yell and don't be afraid," she whispered in a sweet southern drawl.

Uko would have ignored her gentle instructions had he not already lost the ability to scream. His shock left him motionless with his jaw ajar.

She chuckled at the silly expression etched into his face.

"I didn't say freeze," she said. "I know this is a lot to take in right now but you're going to be alright. My name is Toni." She reached her slender hand out to him through the darkness. It glowed with life as Uko slowly recovered and returned her handshake.

"How did you get in here," he asked. "Are you one of them?"

"Do I look like I'm one of them? Of course not. I'm a normal person just like you. I just happen to be in this nightmare with you. I know I'm a little late, sorry about that."

Uko shook his head as if it would help loosen the cobwebs that were keeping his brain from processing what was happening. "I'm so confused. I'm making you up in my head right now?"

"Nope. The girl you see is a real person. I'm not a part of your imagination. I'm actually sleeping in my bed at my mom's apartment in Savannah, Georgia. I'm here to help you beat these things coming after you right now. I'm a Nightmare Detective." She trailed off and began speaking to herself, "Well, a retiring Nightmare Detective actually. That's weird to say out loud after all this time."

"Wait. What?" Uko said.

She snapped out of conversation with herself and held his shoulder. Her expression took a serious tone. "Look, I should have been here way before this to ease you into everything. That's on me. Sorry again. But we don't have a lot of time. I'm guessing in a few seconds those skeleton things chasing you will find us in here like they always do, and you'll have to fight. It's going to be really scary, but I'm going to help you. You just have to trust me. Do you trust me?"

Uko was still having trouble understanding who she was, so trusting her seemed like a bit of a stretch. He looked at her hand on his shoulder. It was real and he could feel its weight. She was here, he was in trouble, and she would help. He looked back up at her smiling face. "Yeah, I guess I do," he finally said. "I just have one quick question: How do you kn-"

Before the words could escape his lips, the wall behind them ripped open and a hand of bone sprang forward through the hole. It grabbed Uko's left shoulder while a tangle of more arms burst through the wall to grab Toni. With a violent jerk they pulled the pair back against the wall and then through it. The crash deafened Uko as he was thrown back into his bedroom. He tumbled onto his knees and tried to take in his surroundings. The color in his vision was back in time to provide him vivid detail of the two towering Reapers that stood over him. They stood so close, that Uko could feel the tattered rags of clothing that enveloped them. Thick beads of chilled water dripped off their withered faces and landed on Uko. Fearing he was alone, his eyes darted around the room. Between the skeletons he could see Toni slowly standing to her feet.

"Run, Uko! Follow me," she said as she sprinted out of the room without turning back. The Reapers reached down to impede his movement and Uko narrowly dodged their grip and slipped between them. He smiled to himself for a second, impressed with his agile move. He exited the room and began running after Toni as she sprinted toward the front door. He caught up to her as they exited the dark house and ran into the street. No car or person inhabited the world outside. They ran to the entrance of the park and turned back to the house. If he wasn't aware of what caused them to run out of the house in the first place, Uko would have thought everything was fine. The home seemed peaceful and serene, except for a broken front door. Uko bent over to try and catch his breath.

Toni placed her hands on her hips and laughed.

"That was intense! You've got such a great imagination," she said. "I've always admired that about you."

Uko turned his head to her in confusion. She looked back at him with her beaming smile.

"Right, sorry. I've been in nightmares with you before. Like I said, I'm a Nightmare Detective and our job consists of helping kids who have bad dreams that keep happening," Toni said. She bent down and examined a pine cone on the ground in front of them. She nodded as she spoke. "I've helped you two or three times before. Whoever a detective helps immediately forgets about them when they wake up, so I don't take offense to you treating me like a stranger," she added.

"You've done this with me before?" Uko asked. He was strangely still out of breath. He strained while staring at her as he tried to find something that remind him of the other times they had met. Nothing came to mind. "There are more people like you?"

"Yes, and yes. I can give you details later," she replied. "For now, you gotta get ready to fight. Those skeletons should be coming back soon."

Uko furrowed his brow and pointed to his chest. He shook his head from side to side while mouthing, *Me?!*

"I don't know why you keep saying I need to fight. I have no idea how to fight. I don't even play sports. How am I going to fight those things?"

Uko stood up and noticed that Toni was no longer looking at him. He turned back toward the house. She was staring at a row of skeletons lined in front of the house like a marching band of ghouls. The Skeleton King stood in front of the rest. Even from the distance, Uko could tell he was enormous. He was at least an entire foot taller than the others in his group. Brown and red rags swung from his body and flared in the wind. To his side he held a large staff. The King tapped the staff on the floor and the army behind him marched forward in silence.

Uko turned to run but Toni grabbed his arm. "Don't be afraid. He's you. This is your imagination. You fight him by using your imagination."

Uko looked at her in confusion.

"All you need to do is create what you need to fight an army of skeletons and a creepy, giant skeleton with a walking stick," Toni added.

"Oh, is that all," Uko replied. He shrugged his shoulders. "I thought this would be hard."

Uko looked back at the Reapers and hoped that a solution would come to him, but it did not. They were entering the street now, only 50 or so yards away. He tried to imagine them disappearing and everything being fine. It made no difference. They continued to walk forward. He turned back to Toni. "Seriously, help me," he pleaded.

"No," she said a soft voice. "You can do it."

She turned and looked up and down the empty street before them. "I will say that it's mighty quiet out here. It's like we're the only ones in this entire street. That's weird isn't it?"

Uko squinted at her. "I guess. What does that have to do with this though?"

Toni smiled back at him and raised her eyebrows slightly. "A lot."

Uko turned back to the group as they approached the middle of the street. He wanted more than anything for this to end but could not figure out how to make that happen. At that moment, it was the one thing he wanted most in the entire world. The strong desire reminded him of his first day of fourth grade when everyone had to give a surprise presentation in front of the new class. His mouth had gone dry the second he was told the terrible news by Ms. Gimble. Since he was little, he had always wanted to be able to give great speeches in front of crowds but that never happened. Instead, he would start dripping in sweat and fumble through the entire thing.

For Ms. Gimble's surprise presentation, he happened to be sick and was too occupied with the aches of his body to worry about anything else. To feel better, he occupied himself with thoughts of a perfect day. He envisioned every moment of his presentation going perfectly. In his mind's eye he could see the reactions of each kid laughing at every joke and hanging on to every word. In his elaborate imagination, he was a master presenter. When he was finally called, it was the best he ever did by far. With no other options and Toni telling him to just think of what he needed, Uko decided to try the same technique.

Standing in front of the park with Toni and watching the impending Reapers, Uko began to imagine a perfect resolution to his problem. Instead of wishing things ended, he created a method for its conclusion. He closed his eyes and envisioned every aspect. Even as he heard feet dragging in the street, he continued to build their escape in his head.

He was jolted out of his daydream within a nightmare by the sound of a large tractor-trailer's horn. As he opened his eyes he could see the skeleton army fly into the air as a truck barreled through the group without pausing. The skeletons screeched a collective wail as they were pummeled by the massive truck. The falling bodies vanished as the truck flew by. Unfortunately, The Skeleton King was slightly ahead of the group and avoided the doom of his men. Clusters of rags and bones scattered behind him. After the last of his troop disappeared, The Skeleton King quietly turned back to Uko and pointed at him. The gesture froze Uko to his spot as he imagined what he would have to do now. Thankfully, the Skeleton King disappeared in a great cloud of smoke, leaving Uko and Toni on a once-again deserted street.

For a few seconds, Uko stared at where the Reaper army once occupied the street. Although his mouth was opened to speak, no words found their way out. Finally, Toni placed her hand on his shoulder and Uko turned to her, "I did it! How did I do it? What was that?"

"It was a little sloppy but good enough," she replied. "You're gonna have to work on getting better at it." She put her arm around his shoulder and began walking back toward the house, "This is just the beginning. You're destined for so much more, my friend. You are meant to do this for kids all over the world."

They reached the doorstep of the house from which Uko ran for his life only a short while before. The world that was dark and gloomy when they began the journey was now bubbling with the dim light and excitement of an oncoming sunrise. Somehow, he had turned the tables on a fear that had terrorized him for weeks. All with the help of a girl he didn't recall meeting, but who claimed to have done this for him before. He was sure he must be losing his mind.

Toni continued, "I won't lie to you. The life of a Nightmare Detective can be thrilling, and it can also scare the crap out of you. But it's the best thing I ever said yes to when I was in your position."

While she spoke, Uko stared at the horizon where the sun rose at triple the speed it would normally. Toni ushered him into the house with a light tap on the back.

"You have to want to help people if you're ever going to reach your full potential," Toni said. She paused and bit her lip before speaking again. "Do you want to see how great you can be?"

CHAPTER 3

The Council Meeting

"I REALLY APPRECIATE YOU helping me out," Uko replied, "but I feel like you have me confused with a superhero or something. That's definitely not me." They walked up the stairs and into his bedroom. The damage that the Reaper army inflicted earlier was now completely fixed. Uko walked over to his dresser and picked up his stuffed lion, Kanju. Without turning around, he snuck Kanju into a dresser drawer as slyly as he could. "I'm just a normal kid who had some bad dreams and somehow imagined you in this one and you helped me figure out what to do."

Toni patiently pleaded her case, "Like I said, I'm not someone you came up with in a dream. I'm a real girl who lives her own real life a bunch of miles away. I can join you in your dreams and help you discover how to overcome whatever nightmare you're having. I've done it a couple times before. Once, when we escaped killer clowns and another time was about some girl from your school that you wanted to ask out."

Uko felt heat rush to his cheeks and he quickly dropped his gaze to the floor. He had a feeling Toni might be talking about his crush, Imani, but trying to recall the dreams she spoke about was like trying to see through heavy fog. He could not confirm nor deny that those things had happened.

"If you ask me, that girl was kind of a brat and not worth the trouble but that's beside the point," Toni said. She rolled her eyes before shaking her head and continuing. "I kept coming back to help you because I saw something special in how you thought, how you handled adversity, how you imagined." Uko felt the heat rush back to his cheeks again. "I knew that when I'd turn fourteen, I'd become too old to be a detective, and I'd have to recruit someone to replace me. I chose you months ago and just waited until it was time. It's finally the summer before you go to junior high. It's time now."

Uko looked at her cautiously and considered what to do next. What if she was telling the truth and this girl standing in front of him was not a figment of his imagination? What if she was a real person he could meet in real life? Someone who was somehow sharing a dream with him at this very moment. The timid and practical side of him wanted to end the conversation and immediately wake up to what he knew. The curious part of Uko wanted to press on. Curiosity, of course, won.

"So, you have to find someone to replace you," he asked. "And I will too someday. I mean, if I joined."

"Yeah, that's the way it works. I was recruited by a boy named Mikey the summer before I started seventh grade. As a detective, you begin right before you start junior high and you have to retire when you graduate and you're on your way to high school." As Uko opened his mouth to ask another question, Toni ignored him and quickly continued, "Mikey told me it has to do with a kid's development in their imagination at that age. I guess when kids get to high school things change and they start taking themselves too seriously. They just want to fit in, which sounds awful." The bedroom continued to get brighter as the sun rapidly rose.

"What's the point of being thrown into the dreams of random kids?" he asked.

"To make an impact that I can't in my everyday life. I've met and helped kids from all over," Toni said while she stretched her hands out wide. "Most nightmares are related to something going on in your life and I've been able to help kids figure out a way to get them through it." Toni sat on Uko's bed and looked down at her feet and her voice lowered. "I don't know if I'll ever be able to do something like that again."

Uko sat on the bed next to Toni and she smiled. The room quickly became bright white with sunlight from outside. Things he could see clearly before were now washed out. Toni was now so bright she was difficult to see. Uko was conflicted. The idea sounded interesting, but he wasn't sure if he believed any of it. His mind was surely playing tricks on him. He paused a long while as he tried to come up with a way to say how he felt, but he couldn't. He settled on asking, "How does it work?"

Toni jumped out of the bed and clapped her hands together before pacing the small bedroom. "There's a lot that I would need to teach you, but you get the idea of what we're about." The room filled with rays of bright sunlight. "I don't have the time to explain the details right now because from the looks of things, you're gonna be waking up soon." She squatted down in front of him. "I chose you for a reason and I think you'll be great. This is *your* chance to make a difference. I know you don't have all the information, but are you brave enough to jump off the cliff without seeing what's below?" She stared at him with an exaggerated smile and her fingers crossed on both hands.

Uko thought about this. He thought about his family and Manny and the simple summer he had planned as a Park Ranger. He always imagined what it would be like to take a chance to do something daring; even if it was in some sort of make believe world. The idea was incredible, but the reality was frightening. He looked at her again, her face completely washed away in the sun's light. "That sounds so freakin' dope. But I can't do it. I'm not that person. I'm sorry," As soon as he finished speaking, everything vanished and Uko woke up.

***

The first thing he heard were the sounds of whispered conversations and cutlery clinking on plates. Even though he was a little dizzy as he lay face down in his pillow, he was certain he was awake. He rolled onto his back and looked around only to yell at the unexpected sight of his entire family sitting by his bed. Each person had a plate of food in their hands as they whispered to each other while sitting on the bean bags in his room.

Uko's mom was the first to speak after his high-pitched squeal. "Sorry to scare you, baby. I came upstairs because you weren't responding to me calling you for breakfast. That's when I noticed you were sound asleep, so I called everyone up to see," she grinned from ear to ear as she spoke. "I haven't seen you sleep so calmly in a long time."

Femi chimed in from the back of the room. "It was a once in a lifetime event. Like watching a panda give birth."

"Come on, Femi! Gross," Uko said while looking around. "You guys brought your food in here too?"

"Breakfast stops for no man," Femi replied while spooning a mound of eggs into his mouth.

"How are you feeling, Coco?" Uko's dad asked. "No bad dream this time?"

Uko thought about the small adventure he'd gone through. He thought about Toni and how he'd declined her offer to become some kind of detective. Normally remembering his nightmares was like trying to hold water in his palm and keep it from slipping through his fingers. Today his memory was crystal clear.

"It started as a bad dream," Uko said. He rose from his bed and began searching for the writing pad he kept for the rare occasions he remembered a small part of his dreams. "But then it was alright. I figured it out, I guess."

"That's interesting. I'm glad it wasn't like the others." Uko's dad said as he got up to collect the plates, "I'll see you later, boys. I gotta run to the store for a few." Uko's mom kissed Uko on the forehead and his parents walked out of the room. Femi remained reclined in a bean bag as he grazed on the rest of his pancakes.

In the search for the writing pad, Uko found his phone instead and texted Manny. He needed his confidants in a time like this. He dictated a text into his phone to avoid having to type it out, an annoyance of his.

"Meet me on the benches by the basketball court in an hour. Crazy story. Four in the park!"

"You're calling a Council meeting? What's the crazy story?" Femi asked. "Do you need help deciding which underwear to keep on for the next week?" Femi jokingly added.

"Shut up. Actually, I'm calling the Council for something important. I wanted to get everyone's opinion on a dream I had," Uko said. Before Femi could respond, Uko patted him on the shoulder as he rushed out of the room to get ready. "I'm not telling you anything before we all meet. Gotta save the good stuff." Uko chuckled as Femi begrudgingly knocked his hand off his shoulder.

***

At the park, Uko paced in front of a bench like a lawyer in the middle of a trial. On the bench sat the group he called "The Council." His big brother Femi, his best friend Manny, and Manny's little brother Carlos. These three boys were his closest friends and family, a group he trusted completely. They were the people he came to with life's difficult decisions like what to wear for the first day of school or how to deal with a bully. Whenever one of them needed the help from the group, their secret phrase: "Four in the park", was all that needed to be said. It was like Commissioner Gordon turning on the Bat Signal. No explanation was needed. Wherever they were at: home, school, or at their grandma's house, they gathered as soon as possible and tried to solve the friend's problem together.

One time, Uko called the group together to discuss how he was going to deal with his longtime school crush, Imani; the same girl that he was apparently getting assistance with asking out in his nightmares. Imani was captain of the girls' basketball team, easily the prettiest girl in the school, and extremely popular. She was essentially perfect and had to fight boys off with a stick. Once, during a science class they had together, Imani chose Uko to be her lab partner. Uko was his usual stuttering, sweaty-palmed-self around her but afterward he hoped that this was a sign. Maybe she was tired of the cool kids and wanted to hang out with him from now on. He sent "FOUR IN THE PARK!!!!" to The Council's group text and they met on the playground right after school. The group wisely advised Uko that she probably just chose him because Imani's best friend was absent that day. But still, you gotta keep hope alive.

Now that it was the summer, The Council was only called from time to time and for special occasions since life crises normally don't happen outside of the school year. Today was one of those rare occasions.

Although Uko hesitated a bit because he feared sounding like an idiot, he presented The Council with what happened. He never had a dream remain so clear in his memory for so long the next day, so the storytelling was easy. The boys thought he was joking at first, but quickly realized how serious he felt about what he went through. They listened attentively and remained silent when he finished. He stood frozen in place in front of the park bench and awaited their feedback.

He could feel a familiar squirming in his stomach—the same squirming he'd felt each of the million times he'd thought about Toni's invitation. He looked at their faces as they quietly sat on the bench, trying to read their expressions. He considered saying he was joking about the entire thing as each second of silence passed.

Manny's brother, Carlos, was the first to speak.

"So, you're telling me that you actually believe that this girl is real? Are you serious?"

Carlos had a way of sounding rude even when he didn't mean to be. He was easily the most argumentative fourth-grader in his elementary school, and he had his fair share of detentions for arguing with teachers about things he didn't agree with. Being able to hold his own in a debate made it easier to hang out with bigger kids like his older brother Manny's friends. In The Council, he was the person who cut through small talk and said what everyone else was too polite to say.

"Is that crazy?" Uko replied.

"Yes, it is," Femi said, "I'm glad you asked. It is crazy."

"It's not that crazy. People don't know all there is to know about everything in the universe. Scientists are still finding out stuff about the world. Maybe this is something smart people don't know about yet," Manny added. Typical Manny—always the peacemaker. Uko loved that about him, especially on a day like today.

"Manny, come on," Carlos responded, "you don't make any sense."

"I get it, guys. It sounds made up. But something about the entire thing was different. It was like she knew me but not well enough to be someone I created myself." Uko began pacing again and waved his arms while he tried to find the right words. "Even though everything was all over the place with the skeletons and stuff, I still had this feeling like I was still a little in control. I kinda knew what they would do next. But with her it didn't feel like that. She did what she wanted." He looked back at their faces when he finished and saw blank stares. He sighed and sat on the bench as Femi got up to walk around the group.

"Let's just assume she's real," Femi said. "What should I-"

"If she's real and what she said was real then you said no is because you were being a punk," Carlos interrupted. He was being a little rude on purpose this time to make a point. "You're afraid to take chances on anything and this is a perfect example."

The group stared at Carlos as he rose to clarify. He was saying something they'd each felt at separate times about their friend Uko, so no one dared mess up the moment with even a cough.

"Get 'em," Manny whispered as he broke the silence. Uko shot his eyes at him.

"Relax, guys. I'm just saying," Carlos said as he stood in front of the group, "you gotta admit that at least, Uko."

"I don't know about all that," Uko said. He leaned back and looked to the sky as he thought of examples that would disprove Carlos' point. "But what does that have to do with Toni anyway?"

"Are we taking this stuff seriously?" Femi interjected. "Tell me I'm not going crazy. Uko's making created players in his head and we're callin' Four in the Park?!"

"Speak on it," Manny said as he nodded. Uko sprung up from the bench. He pointed at Femi, but couldn't come up with words to go with the gesture.

"If my man says it happened, then it happened," Carlos quickly said. "That's not the point. The point is," he added while taking a deep breath. "You're scary. About everything."

Uko sucked his teeth. "No, I'm not!"

"Yes, you are," Femi replied.

"You remember that checkers tournament a couple of months ago at school?" Manny asked.

Uko took a little longer than usual to reply because he knew where the story was going. "Yeah."

"I had to drag you to it because you said you never played and didn't want to look bad in front of everyone. I kept telling you it wasn't that hard to learn, but you wouldn't listen. When I finally got you to play, you ended up making it to the finals," Manny added.

"I still lost to Angelica," Uko responded.

"Angelica is a beast. That was expected, man. That's not the point. You scary," Femi replied.

Uko looked from Femi to the rest of the group. He sucked his teeth again before turning his back and looking out into the park. After a slight pause, he turned back to them.

"So, I should find Toni and say I want to join the squad," he said.

"She's not real though. We just wanted to tell you about yourself." Femi laughed.

"She is real," Uko pleaded.

"Okay then," Manny said to stop an argument before it started again.

"You believe me, right?" Uko asked Manny.

"I just wanna play some ball. How about we do that? Uko, you can dream about playing better," Carlos said as he got up and walked toward the basketball courts.

Each remaining member of The Council patted Uko on the back as they walked past him toward the court to join Carlos. He half expected this to be the outcome of their conversation. The Council always seemed to deliver what you needed instead of what you wanted. They may have not completely believe what happened, but they helped him out anyway and Uko appreciated that. He walked behind the group to the courts as he considered everything they said.

"You swear you're so funny, Carlos."

CHAPTER 4

Second Shot at Glory

THE COUNCIL spent the rest of that day running through Newark's largest park like kids enjoying their last day of freedom. After aimlessly shooting around for a while, Femi convinced them to play a pickup game against some reluctant high school kids. Femi was the only one on their team who could shoot, so they lost badly. They still had a great

 47

time going down in flames. Afterwards, Carlos treated the gang to a loser's buffet at the corner store full of powdered donuts, chips, chocolate candies, and 'quarter water' juices. They ate it as a group by the pond while Uko and Manny introduced them to the turtles they ceremoniously named a few days ago.

***

As he prepped for bed that evening, Uko went over The Council's diagnosis. Not long after going to bed, his sleep was interrupted by an annoying knock at the door. He was too tired from a day spent running around to get up and see who it was. Instead he rolled over and closed his eyes again.

The second round of knocking was even louder.

Uko's eyes shot open and he yelled in frustration. All the time spent enjoying the day could never help him escape his nighttime terror. His irritation prickled his skin as the replay of Reaper invasions played in his head.

He shut his eyes tightly and yelled from his bed, "Go away!"

The knocking stopped.

Uko opened his eyes again. Maybe that worked. Maybe it was that easy. Maybe all he had to d-

"No!" a voice shouted from outside the door. Before he could register the shock from such a stern reply, Uko heard the door tear open and the drum of Reapers bursting in for a raid. He hurried to his bedroom door. His feet and legs drenched in the familiar flood of water that soaked the carpets.

"No, no, no. Not again," he said as he ran into the hallway toward his parent's room. His sprint came to a dead stop as he saw that his path was blocked by two menacing Reapers. Thick beads of water dripped from their bones and onto the floor as they approached. Their tattered cloaks gave them an even larger appearance. They both pulled their hoods off and locked their fiery eyes on Uko.

Remembering last night's close encounter, Uko ran toward the pair and ducked with the intention of slipping between them. Unfortunately, the tactic did not have the same effect. The icy hand of one of the Reapers reached down and grabbed his shoulder as he nearly passed through the billowing cloth of their robes. He could feel the grip searing his skin as their fingers tightened.

Uko's vision blurred as he stared at the skeletal hand. The Reaper lifted Uko to its face and laughed.

"That doesn't work anymore," it hissed through a clenched jaw.

Uko struggled to free himself, causing more pain in the process. "Let me go," he yelled as he gripped the skeleton's hand, lifted his legs and kicked the Reaper in its chest with all his might. The thrust broke the hand's hold on his shoulder and he tumbled backward over the railing that overlooked the foyer. He crashed one floor below on his back, causing a breath stealing crunch that left him dazed. If his lungs still had air, he would have howled in agony. Instead, he moaned and twisted as he stared at the ceiling.

His view was obscured by the upside-down face of a girl standing over him.

"Toni," he mumbled as her face became clear. For the first time since the nightmare began, he felt like he could breathe again.

"You already know," Toni replied while she smiled. She reached down and lifted Uko up. His back protested with sharp twangs of pain. He yelped as she roughly pulled him toward the open front door.

"I can't walk. I think my back might be broken or something," Uko yelled.

Toni draped Uko's arm over her shoulder and they hobbled toward the door. "Try not to focus on the pain. Think about how you would walk if your back was fine," she told him as they exited.

***

The sight that greeted them was nothing like the deserted street that was there the last time they ran from Uko's house. This time every inch of street, sidewalk, and park seemed to be covered with people. Their faces were vague yet familiar. They hustled back and forth between each other, no one seeming to be aware of anyone else. People bumped into one another obliviously, recovered, and then continued walking to some unknown destination.

"It's not working. My back still hurts," Uko complained. "Why does it hurt so much this time? I've gotten hurt in bad dreams before but it wasn't like this."

"When I told you about becoming a detective and you created that truck to get rid of the skeletons, something happened," Toni said as she tried to maneuver through the crowd while pulling Uko. He winced with pain from the rude bump of each passing person. "Normally people who decline an offer to join the squad never remember anything once they wake up. They go back to their normal lives. But it looks like you remember what happened and your mind is kickin' things up a level. Like it's taking everything in your dreams more seriously."

Uko pulled his arm down from Toni's shoulder. The mob of familiar strangers continued to hustle in all directions. His back still hurt, but he figured it couldn't have been that bad of a fall. He focused on the crowd around him and the sharp pain began relaxing into a dull ache. Suddenly, someone screamed and that singular scream immediately turned into a chorus of people yelling.

The crowd that had moments before been power-walking in random directions now stampeded away from Uko's house and toward the park behind the two of them. The mass of people shoved Toni, Uko, and each another as they scrambled to get away. Toni and Uko pushed people to the left and right of them to avoid being trampled. Through the crowd, Uko could see the cloaks of the hooded Reapers spill out of the house and charge through the crowd toward them.

"Uko, we have to go. Now!" Toni yelled. She tried to shield herself from the onslaught of charging bodies. The hairs on Uko's arm stood on edge at the sound of panic in her voice. Toni put her hand out for him to grab. Uko sensed something in Toni's expression that was more than just worry. He sensed a need to protect—as if she had to save him from the Boogie Man. Visions of Manny and The Council calling him out for always being afraid flashed before him. He pointed back toward the house.

"Let's go this way," he said.

"What?" Toni asked. "You want to go back to the house? Why?"

"Because what's the point of running anymore," Uko replied, "I'm tired of running."

The stampeding crowd continued to scream as they fled toward safety. The Reapers continued to silently dash through the crowd, looking for their prize. Everyone was playing their part in the madness. Uko, with Toni not far behind, did his best to separate the stream of bodies between him and his fear. His only plan was a hope that by the time he reached a Reaper, he would come up with a plan. That was enough for him. Toni followed. They ducked their heads and charged forward.

Uko and Toni fought valiantly against the waves of people that never lost steam as they slammed against them. The constant charging through individuals who didn't mind being moved against their will caused Toni to look at Uko and laugh.

"We're parting the Red Sea of people," Toni said and moved a screaming boy out of her way.

"Right. Let's see how fast we can go," Uko replied. He put his head down, stretched out his arms, and ran forward like a battering ram. Toni laughed louder and followed suit. "Oh, my God, look at you!" she said. As they picked up steam and leaned as far forward as they could, the crowd suddenly disappeared. The street they were slogging through full of screaming people became a quiet meadow full of grass.

The sudden change caused them to fall forward on to soft grass. Uko lifted his head from the ground and looked to Toni in amazement. She raised her head and playfully spit a clump of grass onto Uko. Uko laughed. Toni wiped a few blades of grass from his cheek. As she did, Uko's eyes dropped to her hand and the beautiful gold bracelet on her wrist.

"What happened," he asked. Toni looked at her own hand and pulled it away before she spoke.

"Um, you weren't scared anymore. I'm guessing your mind got bored and changed the scenario." She stood up and placed her hands on her hips. "No more running people, just grass stains on my teeth." Toni chuckled as she pulled the remaining bits from her mouth.

Uko stood up while Toni cleaned herself up. He was not ready for such a tranquil moment after pushing through a swarm of people. The meadow was perfect stillness. There was no wind, no rustling leaves or swaying grass. There were no animal squawks or squeals.

"So that's how I get the bad dreams to stop. I just try to come back to this empty field area," Uko asked.

"There are a lot of things that can make a nightmare end but forcing yourself to stop dreaming isn't one of them," Toni replied. "Your mind is gonna do what it wants and if it's having fun creating the world of a really scary nightmare, it'll just keep going. Sometimes you figure out what's happening and try to stop it. That'll just make you think of ways to keep the nightmare going." She spoke slower as she turned back to Uko now that she was clear of grass. Uko felt her watch him as he absent-mindedly brushed himself off. "There have been so many times when I've told myself, 'This is a nightmare, just wake up,'" Toni continued. "But my mind will come up with new reasons about why this time things are real, and just like that I'm right back where I started." Uko did not respond when she finished.

"That's interesting, right?" she added while raising her voice a little.

Uko only half-listened. In his head he replayed his conversation with The Council. "Who's scary now?!" he thought. He might have blown his first opportunity, but no one could deny that he attacked things head on this time and won.

"Awesome," Uko said triumphantly to himself. Toni looked away from him and shook her head. She brushed her chin before speaking again.

"Being a detective means you get access to dreams and nightmares outside of your own," Toni continued. "You get introduced to Pangea."

Uko's snapped his attention back to Toni. "What's Pangea?" he asked.

"It's the world we all share in our sleep. The same way the world started as one great, big continent that was connected called Pangea. While we sleep, we're all connected to each other. Becoming a detective means you learn how to jump through those links."

"Dope! So why did you come back to me even after I said no."

"Your 'no' wasn't strong enough to me. People have to give me a really good reason to settle for a no."

"I think I know what I want now," Uko replied.

"Well, excuse me. Is that so?"

"Yup," Uko replied. He strutted forward like a superhero and turned back to Toni with his balled fists on his hips. "I want to join the detectives."

Toni's smile spread from ear to ear. "I knew it," she said laughing a bit at his theatrics. "I knew you couldn't go back to being the same kid you always were. You've got too many incredible things left to accomplish."

"You think so?" Uko said. He felt a warm feeling wash over him.

"I know so," she replied.

Uko smiled. "So, let's do it then."

CHAPTER 5

The Survival Scrolls

UKO WOKE UP IN HIS BEDROOM to the sight of his stuffed lion, Kanju, staring at him from his dresser. Under normal circumstances, seeing his only stuffed animal was a welcome greeting after a night of tossing and turning. But he would rather be in the meadow with Toni. "She's cool," he thought to himself. She might not be as cool and perfect as Imani, but she was solid. She made him laugh and she found him funny. He liked that about her. Unfortunately, because the dream ended so suddenly, he would have to go an entire day with all of his unanswered questions.

At the breakfast table that morning, Uko replayed the dream over and over in his head. It was as clear and complete in his mind as any memory from real life. He thought about coming face-to-face with the skeleton crew again and standing up to them. He replayed the moment he and Toni stood in the meadow and Uko accepted his calling. He was concentrating so much on these thoughts that he didn't notice how weird he looked staring at a blank wall while he ate.

"Coco, what on earth are you looking at?" Uko's mom said as she turned around and saw him.

Femi and Uko's dad lifted their heads from their phones to chuckle as Uko was snapped back to reality. Uko laughed as well. He figured he must look foolish.

"Sorry. I was just daydreaming," he said.

"I hope you were daydreaming about the Lit Fest today. You and your brother are coming to help me this time," she replied.

Shoot! Uko forgot he and Femi promised they would help their mom volunteer at the library. He groaned to himself at the thought of all the work involved and being on call with his mom all day. Other than that, he loved Lit Fest! The second Saturday of every month, the local public library hosted Newark Literary Festival, a day filled with interactive puzzles, games, and mini plays-all inspired by popular books. Kids from all over the state came to eat Cat in the Hat cookies and King Aslan brownies while they watched volunteers in goofy costumes recreate scenes from their favorite books. It was an event that Uko's mom lovingly started years before when Femi was just a baby. Sometimes Uko and Femi joked about which thing their mom loved more—Lit Fest or Femi. Depending on the day, Femi would be a close second.

Although Femi and Uko loved eating the snacks, playing the games, and watching the silly sketches, they usually didn't get time to do any of the activities when they helped their mom. They typically spent the day hustling between rooms making sure everything was running smoothly. From time to time, they explored the rarely used offices in the old building. The dusty rooms stacked with old books and newspaper clippings felt like they held the secrets of the city.

"Can we invite Manny and Carlos?" Uko asked.

"Sure. If they're free, I'd be happy to bring them," Uko's mom replied.

The ride to the library in the family minivan was filled with hushed excitement. Manny, Carlos, Femi, and Uko huddled in the backseats while Uko retold the story of his latest dream. When he was done, Carlos was the first to chime in.

"Congrats, man," he said. "You finally put your big boy pants on."

Femi shifted in his seat and sighed loudly. Manny turned to him in annoyance.

"Relax, Femi," he said.

"I don't care what he thinks," Uko said. He forced a smile to prove his point. On the inside he screamed at his brother for never hearing him out. "He's just upset that it's happening to me and not him."

Femi scoffed and looked at the other boys. They looked back at him with serious expressions. "Ok, let's just assume this is real," he said. "Why can't you find us when we're sleep?"

"I don't know, man," Uko replied. "I don't even think I'm officially a detective yet. I just said yes and then I woke up."

Femi leaned forward and placed his hand on Uko's shoulder. "I bet they gotta jump you in like a gang. That's really gonna pretend hurt," he said through choking laughter. Uko slapped Femi's hand from his shoulder.

"Ow," Femi mockingly screamed.

"Settle down back there, boys," their mom said from the driver's seat.

"Let's just change the subject," Carlos said to the group in a calming tone.

"Whatever," Uko said while turning to the window he sat next to. He stared out and people-watched as a way to calm down. There was a moment of quiet tension.

Manny broke it by telling the group his plan to make an adventure out of this month's Lit Fest. After trying and failing a few times before, today they would search the library for a lost Black Panther comic book they'd been hunting down.

A few months ago, Femi had searched the library's online catalog and found out that it stocked a rare issue of the comic. He searched the shelves for days, but couldn't find it. He eventually gave up, but Manny swore that the comic had to be somewhere in the building. He figured it was probably lost years ago, collecting dust in a forgotten storage closet. They searched room after room for several Saturdays but never came across it. Today, Manny convinced everyone to give it one more shot after hearing that a new Black Panther video game was in the works. If they could find the comic, they could finally read it in all its glory.

"What do y'all think," Manny asked. Each boy replied with a lighthearted OK except for Uko.

"What about you, Uko?" Manny asked.

"Isn't that Derek?" Uko asked in reply. As their car was stopped in traffic, Uko pointed at a boy playing in the water spraying from a fire hydrant across the street.

"Yeah, that is him," Femi said as he leaned over Uko to see. "Is he still in our school? I haven't seen him in a minute."

"Who cares. Look at his shorts!" Carlos jumped in to say.

"Let me see," Manny said as he slid over to Uko's window.

Derek ran around the hydrant with two other boys and a girl who looked a little younger than everyone in the group. He was shirtless and had on bright pink swim trunks with green flamingos stamped all over them. He couldn't hear Uko and the boys burst into laughter from inside their minivan.

"He can't be serious," Femi howled.

"Be nice," Uko's mom called back to them in a stern voice.

They partially calmed their laughter as they watched Derek frolic in the water. He cupped his hands to gather as much as he could and tossed the water on the girl while she sat on the curb with her back to him. She jumped up in protest and chased after him. He screamed in laughter and began running down the block away from her. He crossed the front of two small houses before turning back to taunt her when she stopped chasing. When she broke into a run toward him again, he back pedaled past the next house that had big bushes blocking the front lawn. As he crossed the bushes into the home's driveway, a black car suddenly appeared as it sped toward the street. There was no way for Derek to hear the boys scream from their huddle in the back of the minivan. He turned in time to see the car and put his hands out toward it. The driver of the car saw him in time to slam on the brakes, causing a loud screech to rip through the quiet street. But before it could come to a full stop, the car slammed into Derek and tossed him over its hood and roof. He disappeared behind the big bushes before the car came to a stop at the end of the driveway.

Uko's heart pounded so fiercely and abruptly that he thought he may have been hit himself. The screams of his mother, the rest of the guys in the car, and the people outside sounded miles and miles away. He could only hear the screech of the brakes ring in his ears and the thumping beat of his heart. He felt as though he was stuck in mud as everyone emptied out of his car and rushed toward Derek. He stayed in the van, fighting to catch his breath and quiet his heart. It wasn't until an ambulance arrived several minutes later that Uko felt closer to normal. His mom and Femi spoke with an officer about what they saw while Uko stared at them from the same window. When everyone finally returned to the car and they continued their drive to the library, Uko's heart had relaxed. But that screech still tinged his hearing.

After a somber drive, they finally got to the library to find that there were already dozens of kids with their parents already lined up waiting for the event to start. Volunteers rushed back and forth as they assembled Katniss Everdeen cardboard cutouts and banners. The spectacle that normally thrilled Uko had a weird vibe to it after what he had just witnessed. The boys walked past the Sherlock Holmes-themed table in the middle of the library's foyer and gathered in front of a small coat closet to put their things down before starting the day's work.

"We don't have to look for the comic if you don't want to Uko," Manny said as they placed their things away.

"Why wouldn't we look," Uko asked.

Femi looked at Manny and Carlos with a worried look in his eye. "Because of Derek," he said. "I know you needed a second after it happened."

"I'm good," Uko said to him. He kept his eyes on his book bag while he zippered pockets that didn't need to be closed. "You don't have to worry about me."

Femi looked back at Carlos and Manny.

"Nah, we're not saying we're worried," Carlos said. "Just saying we don't have to look for the comic today. We could just focus on helping your moms out."

"I'm good guys," Uko said. He gritted his teeth as he thought back to the image of him freezing in the van while everyone else rushed to action. "Let's find this comic."

Carlos looked at Femi who shrugged his shoulders in reply.

"Ok man," Manny finally said.

"Carlos and I will be working with my mom on the second floor. So, when we're free, we'll search that floor for the book," Uko told the group. "Femi and Manny, since you're helping with the plays on the fourth floor, you guys search up there. We haven't really looked through those rooms yet so make sure you take your time and check everything twice."

"Looks like you got it all figured out," Carlos replied.

"Of course," Uko said.

The boys looked at each other in silence for a moment. "We got it, Captain," Femi finally said while saluting. "I'll text the group if I come across anything interesting."

"Just in case we lose service or something," Manny said as he looked at his phone, "let's meet here at 2 o'clock to update everyone on what we found."

"Sounds good," Uko replied. He clapped his hands and smiled. For a second, Uko thought he heard one of those miles away screams again. He ignored it and waved to the boys, "Let's get it." The group separated and headed to their respective floors.

Uko and Carlos spent much of the early afternoon busy with Lit Fest activities. When the two finally did get some time to search for the comic, it was almost one in the afternoon. They started their search in a dusty room next to an old computer lab. Both boys rummaged through box after box, but couldn't find anything more interesting than a stack of faded, old newspapers. Next, they tried their luck in another room with worn out library books. This proved to be just as useless as their first attempt and Uko nearly called the search off before his and Carlos' phone buzzed with a group text from Femi:

"Found something cool. Come to fourth floor."

Carlos and Uko smiled at each other and they both hurried to the room where their assigned group of Lit Fest attendees were finger-painting Charlie and the Chocolate Factory coloring books.

"Guys," Uko said in a voice so loud it startled everyone in the room, "Sorry for the interruption. Um, we're going somewhere. We're going upstairs to get something. We'll, uh...we'll be back." Uko was never very good at coming up with white lies on the fly.

The boys ran out of the room to the floor's old elevator, smashed the UP button, and waited impatiently as it sauntered its way up to them. They hated having to wait for something so rickety and painfully slow, but the fourth floor was only accessible by elevator.

"Manny was right all this time. The comic really is still in the building. I'm so hyped," Carlos said as they waited.

"I know," Uko replied. "I told you we should still look for it today." His excitement and impatience made him sway from side to side as if he were in a long line for the bathroom. "Hopefully, it's in good condition. I want to read it but if it's in really good condition, we shouldn't even open it. We should just preserve it."

The boys rushed into the old elevator and rushed back out when it arrived at their destination. The floor was empty, but they could hear commotion from one of the rooms down the hall. As they looked through the door's window, they saw kids laughing hysterically as Lit Fest volunteers acted out a silly version of the book

Dracula. Uko scanned the room for Femi and Manny, but couldn't find them in the crowd.

"They're not in there," Uko said.

"We should have asked where they were when we got the message," Carlos replied, "I'll text 'em back."

"PSST," whisper-screamed a voice from down the hall.

Carlos and Uko turned to see Femi leaning outside a door with a ridiculous grin across his face. They jogged over to him while Femi looked up and down the hall repeatedly.

"Can I help you boys with something," Femi sneakily said as Uko and Carlos arrived.

"Stop playing, Femi," Carlos said as he pushed by him into the room, "What did you guys find?"

Femi put his arm around Uko's shoulder and guided him and Carlos through the empty office. He waved his free hand in the air like a circus ringmaster while he spoke.

"We searched far and wide, high and low. To the ends of the library and back. I thought we'd never make it," Femi said as they walked through a door in the back of the office. "At one point, I started a diary to document my journey. It was the least I could do."

"Femi!" Both Uko and Carlos screamed to shut him up.

Femi threw his hand over his heart and pretended to be insulted. "Well excuse me," he muttered.

They stepped into a large supply room full of boxes. The floor was covered in a thick blanket of papers, books, and comics. In the middle of the room, Manny sat cross legged as he emptied out a box and searched its contents. He was so occupied with the task that he didn't look up as the group entered.

"We found comics, my friends. Dozens and dozens of comics. Although I will admit we got a little carried away with the unpacking," Femi said as he looked around the room.

While Manny sat in the center of the room, around him was a small mountain of different comics mixed in with school textbooks. The mountain would grow as Manny picked through a box and tossed the undesirable books beside him. After being in his own world for a few minutes, Manny finally looked up and noticed everyone staring at him.

"Oh, hey, Uko. Hey, Carlos," Manny said. "We struck gold! Carlos, come help me sort through this. Uko, you should start with those boxes in the back."

Uko gladly jogged to a stack of untouched boxes in the back of the room. He pulled one down from the top and tore it open as he sat. The box was filled with an assortment of moldy comics along with a tattered composition notebook which he pulled out. On its cover was a large white box intended for a student to label the contents. Uko read the label aloud to himself.

Name: The Oral History of Pangea
Subject: Volume III

Uko nearly dropped the book and gasped. He brought the book closer to his face and read it again to be sure. "Pangea," he whispered to himself. "Oh, my God!"

"You find anything good?" Femi called to him. The sentence briefly interrupted the shock Uko felt from reading the cover. "Pangea," he muttered to himself again. It was the same name that Toni used to describe the world of dreams.

"I just found an old notebook," Uko said a little louder as he opened it and began reading.

The history of man is written by the few, but the history of dreams must be told by the many. For nights on end I wandered the stretches of Pangea in search of new people to meet. This is my collection of conversations with the young and the old about their experiences in this world. Some I've come to call friend, while the memory of others will terrify me 'till my final day. Regardless of what brought them to the decisions they've made, their stories are important. I pray that future generations will learn from our collective mistakes.

~ The Griot

Uko jaw dropped while he tried to process what he held in his hands. He flipped through it and saw page after page of writing. Each block of text was headed with a person's name, a date, and time. The headings had to be the names of the people they met and the times they spoke with them. It was like Uko's dream journal at home—only much, much cooler.

"Come on, put that mess down and keep looking! We're this close to finding the greatest comic ever and you're over here reading old school notebooks?" Femi chimed in from over Uko's shoulder.

"This is about Pangea," Uko replied. "That dream I told you about. The girl called the world Pangea. This is a journal of stories from people in Pangea," Uko rapidly said. "I told you I wasn't crazy. Whoever wrote this has been there too." He handed the book to Femi, confident he proved his point. "Read one of them."

"I'll read it later. Stop wasting time," he said.

"This ain't a waste of time!" He opened the book to a random page. "Listen to this."

Harris Baldwin   September 8th, 1986   7:03AM

It happened one night a couple years ago. I was dreaming about being in my favorite coffeehouse. I remember sitting by the window with a piece of paper and black coffee just like I do every day when I'm awake. The whole place was empty and I was sitting there staring out the window minding my own business. Suddenly this beautiful young lady appeared out of nowhere, sat across from me and said, "You should own this place."

That's how it started. She visited me every night for a week after that. Every time it was a new lesson. Building things, jumping dreams, slowing time, meeting other people—just so much. It was incredible. I'm an old man who's seen his share of things in life but that was a special time for me.

Every time I slept, I went right to that coffeehouse. I'd sit at my table and my friends would appear. Guys I haven't seen in years, friends from school, people I used to work with. They would just walk in the door and say hi and have a seat. And it was them, you know? Not a version of them that I imagined. It was really them sitting there. It's hard to describe how much that changed my life. We'd talk and talk about life and the good ol' days and our grandbabies and all of that. We'd laugh together over silly jokes. We'd cry together when times were rough. We were a real community and only a couple of us lived near everyone else in real life.

When I first learned about Pangea I did some exploring but that coffeehouse is what I'm gonna miss most. That and Esmeralda, who taught me about Pangea. She gave me everything I needed to be happy again. She told me I could own that place and sure enough, I did.

"Come on!" Uko said triumphantly. The others turned to see what the commotion was about. "Do you realize what this is?" Uko asked as he read the different names and dates. "Someone wrote about the people they met while they were in Pangea, the dream world. It's a journal. If this doesn't prove what I've been saying, I don't know what else will."

Femi looked from Uko to the group and then back to the book without speaking. "No, it's not," he finally said. "You probably came up with that story after reading this."

"When would I have read it?" Uko asked.

"I don't know when. You probably had us come here to discover it, so you can pretend to prove your point," Femi responded. "That's why you were so determined to look for the comic today."

"What are you guys talking about?" Carlos asked.

"Femi, you guys found this place. You told us to meet you here. You don't make any sense. I didn't even know this room existed before today," Uko said. His voice got louder as he became more passionate. "Why can't you just admit that I'm not making it up?"

"Guys, shut up," Manny whispered.

"I'm not saying you made up the whole thing," Femi replied. "You probably did have a dream where you saw all those things. But that doesn't mean that those are real people you met or whatever you think happened. It probably just feels that way," Femi shot back.

"Are you serious?!" Uko exploded.

"Stop!" Manny yelled. "You're gonna get us caught!"

At that moment, the door swung open and a tired looking man in a green sweater and blue jeans walked in.

"What are you boys doing in here?" he said as he surveyed the mess they'd made with wide eyes. "Look at what you did!"

The boys stood frozen in shock as he walked through the room looking at the comics thrown everywhere. "You guys are gonna put all of these books back the way you found them." He stopped in front of Femi and Uko. "Do you understand what I'm saying?"

"Yes," everyone said in unison.

Uko took the journal from Femi and walked to an empty desk to set it aside to make sure it wasn't mistakenly packed away.

"Is that one of our books too," the man asked.

"No," Uko said shakily. "It's mine. It's my journal."

"Are you sure?" the man asked. The man walked over to the table and picked up the notebook.

"Yeah," Uko said.

The man looked up from the pages he flipped through. "Who's the Griot?"

"That's me."

"Really?"

"Yeah. It's a nickname," Uko replied. He surprised himself and the boys in the room with what might be his first real lie to an adult.

"What you know about a Griot?"

The man laughed and tossed book back on the desk. "Make sure you guys clear this all up."

CHAPTER 6

This Thing of Ours

AFTER CLEANING THE ROOM, the boys were
forced to return to their Lit Fest duties without
finding the comic. While everyone else was upset
about getting so close without reaching the prize,
Uko was too excited about the Griot's notebook to

care. When he got an opportunity, he could read those stories to learn more about this new world. That made coming up empty on the hunt for Black Panther worth it and temporarily helped him forget about seeing what happened to Derek.

That evening when his mom kissed him goodnight and the house went dark, Uko broke out the notebook from underneath his bed. With a flashlight in hand, he planned to read as much as he could about the lives of other citizens of Pangea. Unfortunately, the long day got to him and he ended up falling asleep shortly after starting.

***

Uko awoke to the sound of birds chirping and the soothing feeling of a warm sun shining on his face. He lifted himself onto his elbows, realizing that instead of being in his bed, he was laying in another dewy meadow. As he looked around to take in the calm sight, his eyes fell on Toni as she stared back at him with a smile and crossed arms.

"Welcome, welcome," she said as they made eye contact. Her curly hair flowed in the wind. Her thin gold bracelet on her left wrist sparkled in the sun, complimenting her deep brown skin as it absorbed the bright daylight. She walked over to him with an outstretched hand to help pull him up. "I was early this time. I've been waiting for you."

"I was worried I wouldn't see you again," Uko replied. "I told my friends about you and they didn't believe me at first. I kinda started to doubt it myself, to be honest."

Toni pulled Uko up and patted him on the back.

"You told your friends about me? That's interesting. I've never told anyone anything about being a detective because I figured that no one would believe me." Toni pointed toward the horizon as a signal for Uko to go with her in that direction and they began to walk. "There's so much that I have to cover with you. I spent the entire day thinking about how I'd get you up to speed. There's no specific handbook we're supposed to use to train new recruits. It's kinda just up to us and we have to help them figure it out along the way. The guy who recruited me, just kinda threw me to the wolves. But don't worry, I won't do you like that."

"Ok, great, cuz that would suck," Uko said through a wide grin. He stared at Toni as she spoke with more focus than he remembered doing before. He figured it was because of how things ended so abruptly last time.

"I found a journal that someone used to write interviews with people they met in Pangea!" Uko excitedly told Toni. "It's the dopest thing I've ever seen."

"Really?" Toni replied. "That does sound cool. You found it in Pangea?"

"No, I found it in the library. I was there with some friends looking through old books, and I came across it," Uko said. He thought about Lit Fest and then remembered the ride there. He shook his head in attempt to push the thought away.

"Nice. Maybe that person worked at the library?" Toni replied. "Read anything really interesting yet?"

"The whole thing is mind-blowing," Uko replied. "Even the simple stuff with people talking about growing a garden in Pangea and how much they loved it."

"Cool. Let me know if you find something juicy. Maybe I can learn some Pangean gossip," Toni laughed. Uko smiled at the sound.

"Do people here have secrets to gossip about?" Uko asked.

"Of course," Toni replied. "Everybody does."

"So that means you do too, right?" Uko added. Toni squinted and smiled.

"Let's get back to business," she replied. Uko's ego swelled at the thought that he might have said a clever thing at the right moment. "Right now, we're in kind of a limbo dream," she continued. "This is basically the lobby that is the in-between of being completely awake and deep in sleep. It's different for everybody. Yours apparently is a meadow with butterflies and stuff." Toni giggled as she mentioned the butterflies. Uko's head immediately deflated. "Mine is a small office with a big wooden desk and some toys in the corner. It's my mom's office actually," Toni said. "When I was little, she would bring me to work sometimes when she couldn't get anyone to watch me. I'd play with the toys in the office and run around till I went home—I loved it." She stopped walking and took in the meadow's beauty. "Your limbo is your happy place."

"I draw sometimes, and I'm really good at drawing scenery. I would do it to relax if I had a bad day or if I got picked on or something," Uko said. He was a little embarrassed at his honesty but continued anyway. "This looks like a 3D version of this magical garden I would draw all the time."

"That's cool, Uko," Toni replied. "I wish I could draw. All I can do are stick figures and stuff like that. Oh, and worms. I can draw the heck out of worm if I just have to make a squiggly line," she added. "I was able to get to your limbo area before you because I have your sleep address. So, I can jump to your dreams or this meadow way easier than if I never met you in Pangea. But, I'll explain that stuff more later on."

The pair walked through the open, tall grass filled meadow toward a group of trees that blotted out the sun above. In the middle of the thickest of trees was a tiny moss-covered path. As they got closer and closer to the path, Toni spoke a little faster.

"Since the beginning of people dreaming, there have been groups who've had strong enough imaginations to control their thoughts even while they were deep asleep. These people would be in a rough dream about something that scared them, and they realized they could figure a way out of it, you know?" Toni said.

Uko pretended to understand and nodded.

Toni nodded back in approval of his supposed understanding and continued, "Then as time went on those same people got better and better at it and would tell other people about their 'gift'. That turned into them teaching people who didn't have the gift how to do the same thing. So, people would travel from far-away places to talk with these gifted people and pay them for the knowledge. Eventually, a lot of fake 'gifted' people started taking advantage of others by charging them crazy amounts of money to pretend to help them solve their nighttime terrors and stuff," Toni added.

Uko wanted to interrupt to ask questions. How did she know this? How did they trick people? What are you like when you aren't recruiting Nightmare Detectives? Instead of asking all of this, he just nodded and tried to think of an intelligent thing to say in response. "After a while, people couldn't figure out the real from the fake and just decided the entire thing was a scam," said Toni.

"So, kids were scamming people," Uko interrupted. He bit his lip after that slipped out as his intelligent response.

"No, they were adults actually. After the scammers messed everything up for the adults who were gifted, there were rumors that younger kids around our age were able to control their dreams. But only kids would believe that another kid had answers that adults didn't so it never went anywhere," Toni replied. "But, one of those kids, his name was Riley, was really good at it and he figured out ways to actually go into other people's nightmares. He discovered what he named the DreamHub. He's the one that started the Nightmare Detectives squad that we have today."

"So, what made him want to start the detectives," Uko asked. "And what makes you good at it? How do you get to be good?"

"Riley was just one of those good kids who loved to help people. So he went around recruiting kids to help other kids like him with their nightmares. They came up with rules like making sure you don't solve the nightmare for the person you help and the rule about having to stop when you get to high school," Toni replied.

"So, you join, and they teach you all this stuff," Uko said. "Sounds like you took classes or something."

"We don't exactly have detective meetings where we share ideas and stuff. It's more one on one sessions with other Detectives. I got recruited by Mikey and when I retire, I recruit one kid," Toni replied. "In the meantime, I meet kids from all over the world and we share our stories."

And when I'm done, I keep the tradition going by recruiting a kid," Uko said.

"You got it," Toni said.

"Have you met other detectives," Uko asked.

"Yeah, I've met some passing through nightmares. Sometimes two of us end up helping the same kid by mistake," Toni replied. "More than one person could help solve a nightmare if they really wanted to. I've seen some Nightmare Detective teams that solve nightmares in groups, but I pretty much work on my own."

They arrived at the beginning of the mossy path through the trees, the entrance to the forest. It was significantly darker here than it was in the open meadow. The sounds of birds chirping and small animals scurrying back and forth were now only a distant memory. There was complete silence as Uko and Toni stood at the base of the path.

Uko noticed the stark contrast between the bubbly meadow and the almost gloomy forest path. "What's inside this forest? Do we have to go through it?" he asked, hoping the answer might be no.

"Yeah, we do. This is the Silk Road. It's your transition," Toni replied. "In your bed right now, your body is falling into a deeper sleep where dreams and nightmares begin to happen. As we walk down this path, we go into that world. I'm gonna hold your hand so you can guide me because it's going to get really dark as we get closer to the end." Uko worked to avoid cheesing too hard at the idea of holding Toni's hand. "When it gets pitch black, you'll know your way through the forest. Even if you don't feel like you know it, you've been down this path a million times before. When we get to the end, I'm going to ask you if you want to join and begin training. If you say yes, that's when this becomes official and we start getting you prepared."

Toni was more serious than normal which made Uko a little nervous. The dark, foreboding path into a mysterious forest didn't help matters.

"What training do I have to do?"

"There isn't any simulation or anything like that where you practice on pretend monsters. The only way I know to train you would be putting you in another person's nightmare and seeing how you do," Toni replied.

Uko mistakenly squeezed her hand at the comment. Uko wondered how she expected him to do in an actual nightmare when he had no idea what he's doing. He was too embarrassed to voice his thoughts.

Toni and Uko stepped onto the mossy Silk Road and began walking into the dark forest. Just as Toni said, things became very dark, very fast. A few steps onto the road and their surroundings became so dark that it would be hard to see your own outstretched hand. Only slivers of faint sunlight made it this deep inside the patch of clustered trees. The road was filled with logs and rocks and it bent and curved in random directions. In some places, the path split into two options, in other places, as many as five. Despite all of this, Uko had an indescribable understanding of how to navigate the darkness. As Toni's reliance on Uko's guidance increased, her hold on his hand grew tighter, but Uko didn't mind.

"So, Riley trained kids to be detectives and it expanded," Uko said. "Sounds pretty good." Uko groaned internally at his weak attempt to continue conversation.

"Well it's good and bad. Not everyone has the best intentions. There were kids who learned how to enter other people's dreams and took advantage of them. It started off with them solving other people's nightmares instead of helping them learn how to do it on their own. Then those kids realized how much power they had and started manipulating other people's dreams to get something they wanted in real life. People started doing things after they woke up because a rogue detective convinced them to do it in a nightmare. If the person resisted, they would keep coming back every night until they gave in."

Uko shuddered at the thought of having a stranger stalk their dreams every night until he gave them something they wanted. He thought about the Skeleton King that he suffered through every night and wondered if he was some sort of undead detective.

"Do those kids still do that now?" Uko asked.

"Yes," Toni answered. "It's not just kids who do it either. There are adults who do it too. They never retire," she added. "They just keep living in Pangea as rogues."

Uko was disturbed by the thought. He didn't realize so much went into this world that he didn't even know existed a few days ago. "That's terrible," he said before kicking himself for another bland response. He thought of something more noteworthy to say and turned to Toni in the dark. "Maybe I can change that."

Toni didn't say anything in reply and Uko kicked himself again for trying too hard.

The pair reached another fork in the road. Uko began walking toward the left option but noticed that Toni had stopped.

"This is the end of the road Uko," Toni said.

As Uko turned back to the path ahead of him, a bright flash of grayish white light streaked in front of him. A sheet of swirling fog hung between the trees where there was only blackness before. Suddenly, dark purple clouds mixed with the gray and silver fog. Through the purple clouds, images rapidly appeared and disappeared in different sections. Uko could see the outline of faces and people, as well as buildings and cars. Every image was tinted with the purple swirls and they moved so quickly he could not make out details. It was like trying to watch a cartoon through television static.

"What is this?" Uko asked.

"This is the DreamHub," Toni replied. "This is where you decide where in the world of Pangea you want to go or whose dream you want to enter. If you know someone's sleep address, this is where you use it to jump to where they are. As you spend more time here, you get better at making out what these random images mean. I first found you while staring at my DreamHub."

Uko stared at his DreamHub's cloudy picture of lavender, silver, and violet. He reached out to touch an image and it wisped around his fingers before returning to the floating sheet of fog.

"This is where you make a decision," Toni said. "I gave you an idea of what you're getting into. If you're still interested, then we would go into your training. A toddler's nightmare. After that-"

"Why a toddler's nightmare?" Uko interrupted.

"Toddlers usually have simpler nightmares—oversized toys, mean dogs, weird monsters. It's easier to figure those out because of how silly they seem when you're not 3 or 4 years old. Let's help some little boy or girl catch the runaway ice cream truck or whatever it is."

"That sounds fine. I'm down," Uko asserted.

"But after this, things get real. Some nightmares are extremely realistic and scary. You can get hurt. Really hurt. On top of that, being a Detective means you don't solve it yourself. You help the dreamer do it, no matter how hard headed they are," Toni added.

"I appreciate you telling me all of this, Toni." Uko took a deep breath and faced the swirling DreamHub again. "I'm in."

"Are you sure, little boy?" she said through a smile.

"Let's go, little girl."

CHAPTER 7

Jurassic Chase

UKO PULLED TONI TOWARD THE DREAMHUB and Toni reached out to grab one of the moving images. The purple colored outline of a large animal turned to them and opened its mouth wide. The clouds of silver and violet reached out and surrounded Toni and Uko and brought them into darkness which eventually gave way to light so brilliant it caused the two of them to cover their eyes.

"I'll never get used to that," Toni said as she stared at the ground.

As the two of them adjusted to the light, they began to take in what was around them. They were in tall grass heavy with wet dew. The air was misty, and an orchestra of animal squeals, calls, and chirps bombarded them from all directions. They were still surrounded by a mob of trees, but these giants were full of life. Their trunks were covered in moss so dense it resembled carpet. All around them lush green vines as thick as ropes swung from tree branches and the leaves of the trees formed a roof-like weave far above Toni and Uko's heads.

"There," Toni said as she pointed across the clearing before them. Fifty yards away, behind a large stone, a young boy squatted with his hands covering his ears. He could not have been more than four years old and was dressed in colorful pajamas with cartoon characters on them. His clothes were in pristine condition even though he was surrounded by wet foliage and muddy grass. His bright white shirt atop his olive colored skin caught Uko's attention as he and Toni approached him. In both of his hands, he held large balls of what looked like socks. As they got closer, they could hear the boy whimpering. He did not notice the presence of anyone else, even as they stood right next to him.

"Hi," Uko asked tentatively, "Who are you?"

"مساعدة," the boy screamed as he whipped his head up at Toni and Uko. "لا تؤذيني"

"We're not going to hurt you," Toni said. Uko looked at her in confusion. He was pretty sure the boy was not speaking English and yet she was responding. She bent down next to him and placed a soft hand on his back. She spoke slowly and used her hands to emphasize everything. "اسمي هو Toni. هذا هو Uko."

She turned back to Uko and he raised his eyebrows.

"I introduced us to him," she said.

"What language is that?"

"Arabic," she replied.

"You know Arabic? When did you learn Arabic in Savannah?"

"Don't try to play me. You act like Savannah's in the middle of nowhere," she said as she playfully punched him in the arm. Uko was surprised by how strong the punch was as he rubbed the pain away. "I learned a little bit while in Pangea. Enough to be dangerous."

Uko made an 'O' shape with his mouth in recognition. "Oh, because you meet kids from different countries?"

"I'm a CIA agent, baby. You can be assigned to the nightmare of anyone who's sleeping at the same time that you are. I meet a ton of kids that speak Arabic. The ones who speak both English and Arabic helped me learn," Toni said. "Now, what do you want to ask him?"

"Oh, um...what does he need?" Uko replied.

The boy looked back and forth between Uko and Toni dozens of times. He furrowed his brow as they spoke.

"He needs your help. He's in a nightmare if you remember," Toni replied.

"I know, I know," Uko said. "I mean what does he need us to do?"

"Is that what you want me to ask him?" Toni asked.

"Yeah," Uko replied.

"I don't know how to say all that," Toni said. Uko threw up his hands in exasperation.

"Umar," the boy said while pointing to himself.

"What?" Uko asked when he realized the boy was speaking to them.

"Umar," he repeated and pointed to his chest.

"He's name is Umar," Toni said sarcastically.

"I get it," Uko replied with an eye roll. Toni smiled in silent reply.

"مـن أي بـلـد أنـت؟" she asked him.

"Cairo," he replied.

"He's from Cairo."

"Interesting," he said to himself.

"That's in Egypt," Toni added.

"I know, Toni!"

"When did you learn that in Newark," she said through a suppressed laugh.

The ground suddenly shook, causing Toni to cut off her laugh. Umar screamed and as Toni and Uko looked at him, he pointed at their feet.

"خـلـع الـجوارب الـخاصة بك," he yelled in a panic.

"What?" Uko asked while looking to Toni for help. She shook her head, letting him know they were in the same position.

"جوارب," Umar repeated while bending down and touching the sock on Toni's ankle. The sound of a large tree boomed, and the ground shook again. Umar began speaking even quicker in long sentences that Uko had no hope to understand.

"Feet?" Toni asked. She turned to Uko. "I'm not sure what he's saying, and this doesn't look good."

Uko's breath quickened as she said that. He looked around them frantically, hoping to see something that would help. Umar pointed to Toni's ankle again then raised the socks in his hands above his head.

"Socks?" Toni asked. She bent down and pulled her sock up and pointed to it. "Socks?"

"Yes," Umar shouted while nodding his head up and down.

Toni turned to Uko. "Take off your socks."

Uko's mind was firing in different directions as he tried to figure out what was happening. Were all nightmares like this? How could he be a detective if he couldn't even figure out what people were saying? He bent down and began removing his sneakers. When he looked over at Toni to see if she was doing the same, he saw her standing with multiple socks in both hands to go along with the socks that were still on her feet.

"I was joking," she said. "You're in a nightmare, just make some socks."

"How do I just make," Uko replied before the sound of an even bigger tree falling cut him off. He quickly removed the socks on his feet and put his shoes back on.

Umar screamed and ran toward the clearing, away from the trees behind the group.

"Uko, let's go," Toni yelled. "We gotta catch up to him. Make sure he doesn't get hurt."

As Toni spoke, Uko focused his attention on the trees behind him. Her words sounded worlds away as he examined the leafy branches violently shaking. He watched a flock of birds fly over their head into the distance. Toni didn't seem to notice the disturbance and took off after Umar. Even though the group expanded their distance in front of him, Uko couldn't move a muscle. The reality of whatever scared Umar so much coming from those trees started to settle into his bones.

"Uko, what are you doing?" Toni called back to him. Uko did not respond, he just stared at the same patch of trees that shook as if they were about to run themselves.

"Dinosaurs," Umar said in terror. He immediately sprinted in a different direction than the one he and Toni had been originally forging toward.

"Umar, no, don't run! Wait for me," Toni called to him. She dropped her socks and ran harder. Her scream to Umar caught Uko's attention and he turned back to the group to see Umar running west toward another line of trees with Toni in pursuit.

"This can't be good for my first test," Uko said to himself as he ran after the group.

Uko caught up to Toni shortly after she reached Umar. "What were you staring at?" Toni asked Uko as he joined.

Before he could respond, her look was no longer on him. It lifted several inches above his head as she caught the view of a massive figure emerging from the spot Uko stared at earlier behind them.

"What the-" she said quietly. "Is that a dinosaur?"

Uko would have turned to see for himself had he not been staring at another dinosaur emerging from the tree line in front of them. It was smaller than the other one, about the size of a baby elephant, with a long neck and a large head. It sniffed the air for a few seconds before swiveling its body and making eye contact with Uko. It had all the characteristics of dinosaurs that Uko saw in cartoons and movies. It snorted as it sniffed, and it let out a deafening roar as its eyes met Uko's. The only thing that was strange about this short and hefty dinosaur was its skin. Instead of the rugged and leathery green or brown skin of typical dinosaurs, this reptile had skin that was paper white. On top of the paper white skin were the broad and colorful strokes of a child's crayon. An ugly mess of purple, green, pink, and red strokes zigged and zagged their way from its head down to its feet. The dinosaur was a child's construction paper drawing. Even the whites of its eyes were scribbled over in a rainbow of random colors.

While Toni took in the massive coloring-book dinosaur behind them and Uko observed the smaller one in front of them, Umar sat with his hands over his head and cried.

"انهم ذاهبون لتناول الطعام لي," he said. Toni looked to Uko for support. It was obvious to Uko that this was the moment she had been waiting for—the first moment of action for him as a new recruit.

"Umar, get up buddy," Uko said and grabbed the boy, his eyes never leaving the festive dinosaur. "We've gotta get you home. Let's go."

Umar sobbed in reply.

"We probably need socks or something like that," Toni added. She was nowhere near as worried as the two boys in the group.

Uko put his hands in his pants pocket and noticed the pair of socks he'd taken off earlier. Umar grabbed one of the socks from Uko's hand and tossed it as hard as he could toward the looming dinosaur. It flew much faster and farther Uko expected. In midair, the dinosaur caught the sock and chomped on it. It lowered its head in concentrated munching. Umar raised his hands over his head in triumph. Uko looked at the remaining sock he held, balled it up, and hurled it at the dinosaur in front of the group. The sock unfurled in midair and floated hopelessly to the ground. The dinosaur ignored this entirely and continued to snort and walk toward them.

"It didn't work!" Uko yelled. He felt himself become more nervous as the dinosaur in front of them crept closer. The one behind them that Umar distracted with his sock was now finished with his meal. He lifted his head and began walking to the group as well, boxing them in.

"Umar needs to do it," Toni calmly stated to the group while she looked at her watch.

Umar melted in sobs and fell to the ground. He curled even tighter into a ball with his hands over his head.

Uko turned to Toni. "We ran out of socks. What's he supposed to throw?"

"You need socks?" Toni asked. "Then make socks."

Uko racked his brain in search of a way to make socks. He had the nightmare with Toni from a few nights before in his head. He remembered destroying the Reapers and tried to repeat the same mental exercise. Before he got far in the process, he felt a brush against his leg as Umar stood up and began running toward the trees to the left of the group. "مساعدة," he screamed as he began his run to freedom.

Uko froze for a few seconds as Umar sloppily stumbled away from him and Toni. The dinosaurs each turned their attention to Umar and began to pursue him. In a few seconds of shock, Uko could see that Umar was right earlier when he said that the dinosaurs were too fast. They were closing in quickly and would easily catch him before he reached the trees.

Uko turned to Toni, unable to do more than project a face that said 'Now what?!'

"Go," she yelled, "Go help him."

Uko turned back to Umar and charged to his defense. The dinosaurs were far enough away from him and close enough to Umar that Uko knew he had to come up with a solution that did not require him to physically catch up to the boy. He began to imagine a solution like he did in his own nightmare.

Uko looked to a large tree at the tree line that Umar was headed toward. He imagined the tree lifting into the air from its massive roots and falling on the dinosaur closest to Umar. He figured this would be his best bet.

The tree wiggled. It even lifted slightly out of the ground, causing dirt and rocks to spill onto the nearby trunks. Uko felt that if he kept at it, he could pull the entire tree up and save the day.

Umar tripped on something in the grass and fell. He turned onto his back and looked up at the dinosaur that had now caught up to him and towered menacingly. Umar screamed with all his might.

"Umar! Get up!" Uko yelled.

His yell echoed as the world around him instantly faded to black and then flashed a blinding white. When the bang of brightness gave way to natural light, Uko saw that he was no longer staring at Umar or the dinosaurs on the verge of attacking him. He was back in his enchanted forest. In front of him Toni sat on a log and shook her head in disappointment.

"Well, that didn't go well, did it?" she asked.

CHAPTER 8

Hail to the Chief

"WHAT HAPPENED?" Uko asked. "Where did everything go?"

"Umar was terrified and he woke up," Toni replied. "When you see that bright flash of light and you're taken back here that means your client woke up. Most of the time it's because they've scared themselves awake. Other times it's something like someone jumping in their bed."

"Umar waking up because he was scared is bad, right?" Uko asked.

"It isn't good," Toni replied. "You gotta remember that they have to figure things out on their own. You trying to solve things yourself is against the rules. It won't work."

"Who made the rules?" Uko asked.

"What?"

"Who made these rules?"

"Riley did when he created the detectives squad. People who don't follow the rules can't be detectives," Toni answered. "We don't want people to rely on us. The point is to teach them to help themselves."

"What happens to you when you can't be a detective?" Uko asked, "You can't go into different nightmares anymore?"

"No. Once you learn how to go into nightmares, we can't take that away from you. Some people don't like the stress of being in other people's dreams all the time, so they just stop and that's fine," Toni said. "Some who didn't want to stop dream jumping ended up forming groups where they can be jerks with other people. But the biggest and most dangerous group call themselves the Coyotes. They're the ones who take advantage of powerful people in their nightmares."

Uko sat on the ground crossed legged as he looked at Toni in a daze. He rubbed his hand over his face. He couldn't even handle himself against a cartoon dinosaur and there's even more evil out there. He wondered who he was to get mixed up in all of this. Why did he think he was brave enough or strong enough or intelligent enough to be a detective?

Toni broke the silence. "You don't have to worry about that, Uko," she said softly. "That's not something we're set up to do. None of the Coyotes are kids. They're adults and most of them have been doing it for years. We stay away from them and worry about helping our clients. If you ever see one, you go the other way," Toni added. Uko didn't reply. Toni squatted in front of him with a look of concern on her face. He felt a wave of embarrassment and frustration flood his body.

"I can't do this, Toni," he finally said without making eye contact. Hot tears welled up as the words left his mouth. He looked to the sky to keep them from spilling out.

"What? Don't say that, Uko," Toni replied. "I know it seems like a lot but-"

"What happens when a detective dies in a dream?"

Toni didn't reply. Uko lowered his head to look at her. He wiped a single tear that trickled down his cheek. Toni still did not reply.

"What happens, Toni?" Uko said. "Tell me."

She opened her mouth to speak then closed it. Then she sighed. "You end up on the Isle of the Dead. Fortunately, I've never been there, but from what I've heard, it's not a good time."

"What is that, an island? You stay there forever?"

"I honestly don't know," Toni said. "I've never died."

Uko felt his skin warm and he clenched his fists.

"I'm not like you, Toni. I can't deal with all of this. I can't learn new languages and jump into scary nightmares and be cool and confident and awesome," Uko said. A second tear trickled down. He didn't bother to wipe it.

Toni moved from her squat to the ground next to Uko.

"Cool, confident and awesome," she said with a slight smile. "That's how you feel about me?"

Uko looked at her and shook his head. "Is that what you heard from everything I just said?" He chuckled. Toni joined him.

"I'm just like you," Toni said. "I'm a regular kid. Things scare me too—all the time. But somehow, I've figured it out. I'm not always perfect, but it's worked out for me. You can do the exact same things I've done. More, actually."

She reached over and wiped his tear. Uko looked at her hand as she did it. Her soft hand warmed his cheek and dried his tears. When she finished, they sat quietly and looked out into the meadow.

"Thank you," Uko said.

"No problem," she replied.

She always seemed to know the right thing to do or say. *Maybe*, Uko thought, *I'll be good at this too someday.*

"So, what do Coyotes look like?" Uko asked.

"They look like regular people. I saw one once when I was training, and he waved at me. Mikey made us leave the nightmare immediately. Never saw one again." Toni stood up and held out her hand to Uko. He cautiously gave it to her and Toni pulled him onto his feet. "I don't want to scare you or anything. It's not like everyone you meet will be bad. I've met a bunch of people in different dreams and nightmares who were really nice." Toni guided him back toward the dark forest and the Silk Road. She walked ahead of Uko and cheerily turned back as she spoke. "Some people just like hanging out doing stuff they can't do in real life." She laughed. "I think I would be the same way if I didn't make it as a detective."

Toni and Uko arrived at the Silk Road. Toni turned to Uko and placed her hands gently on his shoulders. "You don't need to worry about any of that. You're still a recruit. You need to focus on solving your next nightmare. We're not gonna be in practice mode forever. We're gonna go to the real deal soon and you've gotta be at your absolute best. It'll be hard work, but you're gonna make it, kid. I know you will."

Uko felt himself filling with a renewed energy. "I hope so."

"Don't hope. Just know," Toni responded. "I'm going to wake up soon. I can feel it. I'll be back to sleep walking again. That's what we call regular life. The boring stuff. Pangea is where you really get to have fun. But you can go through your forest and go into one of your own dreams before you wake up too. Work on using your imagination and making things do what you want. Be silly and creative. It'll help build your confidence. Tomorrow night, we'll go into another toddler's nightmare and try again. After that, we go to the real deal—a kid your age. That'll be your one and only test for becoming a detective."

"Can't wait," Uko said while pretending to be more excited than nervous.

"You'll be fine. The trick is treating these dreams like a mystery you must solve. The mind can't recreate everyday life perfectly, so every dream or nightmare has something in it that's odd. A detective looks for those things because they hold the secrets to the nightmare. You keep your eyes open and keep your mind alert and you notice more and more of those little differences between Sleep Walking Life and Pangea Life. You'll use those differences to help you beat the bully or slay the dragon."

"Dragons?" Uko nervously asked.

"See you tomorrow night, buddy," Toni replied with a chuckle and vanished into thin air.

Uko stood by himself at the entrance to the dark forest. There was a constant fear of the unknown that haunted him whenever he thought about being an actual detective. It didn't help that Toni seemed to be full of new, dire information to share every time they spoke. Regardless, he was determined that he would press on. He took a deep breathe, clapped his hands together, and stepped onto the Silk Road into the forest.

***

After walking down the pitch-black path, instinctively following the twists and turns, Uko reached the DreamHub again. The gray and purple fog spilled from over his head and onto the floor like a waterfall in front of him. This time, there were no images in the mist. *This must be because I'm by myself now,* he thought as he stepped into it.

The darkness of the forest gave way to another bright light and he squinted until he could see where he was. He noticed that he was still in partial darkness. Looking around he saw that he was on a motionless, unlit subway train. The emergency lightbulbs on the walls of the tunnel were the only source of lighting.

There was no one in the train car with him. Instead, the only things that shared the space were old newspapers that littered the ground. The train sat in silence and abandonment. Looking through the window at the top of the door that led to the next car, Uko could see a faint light flickering in the distance. He slowly walked toward the door, opened it, and cautiously crossed into the next train car. But it was just as the last. The faint glow from the tunnel lights cast creepy shadows as he walked from the back to the front of the car.

As Uko stepped out of a car and crossed the small connector to the next one, he could feel an intense heat while outside. When he stepped back into the car, he would cool off again. His muscles tensed as he stepped outside the train car. When he walked into the next, he held his breath. A few times he thought he saw something move in the train with him and he jumped. It would end up being nothing and he'd sigh in relief and keep moving. After crossing into the fifth car, he paused and sat in one of the dozens of empty seats while trying to understand what was happening. *Is this a test or is it just a random dream?* Knowing how Toni had been spoon feeding him information so far, he wouldn't have been surprised if it was a challenge she'd failed to mention earlier.

He looked around at the emptiness of the train car.

"Hello," he said out loud. "Is anybody else here?"

No response.

He stood and continued his walk to the front of the train. *I'm brave enough. I'm strong enough,* he thought as he moved forward. The flickering light he saw through the front door window was now much brighter and seemed closer. He decided that he'd walk until he got to the light and hopefully it would hold some answers for him. "Toni ain't better than me," he said to himself while grinning.

After walking through a few more cars, he finally reached the beginning of the train. The light was so bright he had to place his hand in front of his face to shield his eyes. He was finally here.

With his eyes squinted, he walked toward the light. It got brighter with each step. So much so that it nearly blinded him. *I should cover the window with something*, he thought. He tried to look around for something but then remembered he was in a dream. Maybe this was a test from Toni. He would have to use his thoughts to cover the window. He imagined the window being covered and it immediately shut closed. He smiled at his accomplishment as he looked down at his hands and imagined himself being a wizard who points at things—causing them to explode or fly in the air. A deep, raspy voice from the other end of the train caused him to snap his head back up.

"Don't you feel like God himself?"

***

The words came from a dark-skinned man sitting, legs crossed, at the far end of the car. Uko yelped. Across the man's shoulders hung multiple brightly colored scarves of different lengths. He draped an old denim jacket over his shoulders, covering most of the scarves. His feet were in dingy neon green socks and pale grey flip flops. Beneath his jacket and scarves, he wore a royal blue Senegalese dashiki gown with crimson red embroidering that flowed to his ankles. Blackout sunglasses covered his eyes. The man rose, grabbed the walking cane that laid across the seats next to him, and approached Uko.

"Do not be afraid," he said as he slowly walked.

Uko stared at him, only now recovering from the shock of it all.

"Who are you," he asked.

"How rude of me. We haven't even introduced ourselves. They call me Chief. You can call me Chief too. Or The Chief if you want to be more formal, which is fine by me. And you are?"

Uko's mind flooded with contradictory ideas. Maybe he should run. Maybe he shouldn't because this was just a dream. There was probably nothing to fear about this man. Maybe there was.

"My name is-"

"Uko, correct? Beautiful name."

"How do you know my name?"

"I followed you into the dream with that little boy in the jungle. I wanted to see what all the excitement was about. We've heard so much about you," Chief replied.

Uko's eyes bulged after hearing this revelation and the casual manner it was shared. He never thought of the possibility of having strangers spying on him in a dream.

"Who are you?" he asked.

"Some friends and I have heard about you. Well not you in particular, but your group. This is the week when Nightmare Detectives get recruited so Pangea is always buzzing with people discussing the new crop. If we have time, my friends like to meet the recruits ourselves while we're out and about. We cross paths with so many people in this world because of our line of work. We're Coyotes." Chief paused and knowingly looked Uko in his eyes. "Are you familiar with who we are?"

Uko's heart dropped. Not even an hour after learning about and being warned never to speak to a Coyote, here stood one just five feet from him. Instead of responding, Uko turned to open the door behind him. Maybe he could walk back into the train car he just came from and this would all be a regular dream again.

"You should really sit down," Chief said. "The train is about to move."

As he finished his sentence, the train jerked forward, tossing Uko into the closed door. The car filled with light and the hum of air conditioners began as the engine came to life. The once calm and quiet train began hustling out of its tunnel and into the bright open air. Uko turned back to Chief and slowly sat in the seat near the door. Chief sat across from him.

"Would you rather the train stop moving?" Chief said. "You can make it stop. You, of course, have control over it. It is your dream after all. I'm just here visiting."

Uko looked from Chief to the door at the front of the train. He willed it and in a few seconds the train came to a complete stop. The air conditioners turned themselves off and the lights died again, leaving the car with natural light from its now outdoor surroundings.

"Very good," Chief applauded, "very good indeed."

"I'm not supposed to talk to you. Please don't hurt me. I'm just going to wake myself up," Uko pleaded. He glanced around as though looking for someone else to help.

"Much easier said than done, my friend," Chief responded. He picked up his walking cane and leaned forward against it. "You don't have to worry about me. I don't want to hurt you. I just wanted to meet you in person. From your reaction, I'm assuming you've heard of my friends, but have you heard of me before?"

"Yes."

"What do you know about me," Chief asked.

"I just know Coyotes are bad people and you take advantage of people in their dreams; unlike the detectives who protect kids in their nightmares."

"No, no, my friend. I didn't mean the Coyotes," Chief said as he placed his open palm on his chest. "What do you know about *me*?"

Uko was confused. Was he supposed to already know about this guy? Was this important info that Toni left out?

"Nothing."

Chief tilted his head back and bellowed a hearty laugh. "Detective propaganda about my group and no history lesson about their leader," he said. "Well today must be your lucky day because not only do you get to meet a brave and mighty Coyote, you get the mightiest of them all. The head honcho. You get to meet me," Chief said before laughing again at the sight of Uko backing up as far as he could to the wall.

He paused to let his remaining laughter subside before continuing. "I saw that girl with you in the jungle—trying to teach you silly made up rules so you can join a worthless group of children. I thought to myself: He looks lost. You looked lost, my friend."

Uko could not think of what to say in response. His thoughts were drowned out by the volume of his heavy beating heart. He continued to look at Chief.

"I was just like you—starting as a nightmare detective and listening to all those lies. All the hypocrisy and greed," Chief said. "It is a privilege to be able to live in a dream; even a nightmare for that matter." Chief leaned back and looked to the ceiling as he spoke, choosing his words carefully. "Most people go through their lives just letting their dreams happen to them. They never get to enjoy the possibilities of what you are now learning. My friends and I don't think that's fair. Coyotes provide a service to the less fortunate who want to live in this world but cannot. For a reasonable fee, we can teach an individual how to live while they dream. How to enjoy Pangea. We can take them from a sad sleep walking life and smuggle them into a world far more interesting."

Chief lowered his head and looked at Uko.

"You agree that everyone's life isn't roses and cute puppies, correct?"

With his mouth open in a goofy gape, Uko nodded. He grew up around people who had far less than he did. His parents constantly reminded Uko of the struggles they both went through growing up. Uko knew and agreed that life could be extremely unfair. Helping people escape didn't seem so bad.

"Now, we can't guarantee that everyone we bring in will be the nicest person once in Pangea. But it is not for us to decide who is worthy. We simply assist. Do you understand?" Chief asked.

Uko's eyes jumped around the train while he nodded his head. While part of him continued to look for an escape, the other half realized this was happening and there was nothing to do about it. "So, you're saying Coyotes don't do anything wrong. It's the people you bring in who mess things up?" he inquired.

"I'm not saying we're perfect. There are still bills to be paid in the everyday world. That may cause a Coyote or two to find ways to make a little extra money on the side through unsavory methods. But it is not as if we are the only ones doing what we must to survive. Some would say that your self-righteous Nightmare Detectives have done more harm than good."

Chief was smooth and calm as he spoke, and it was difficult for Uko to determine how truthful Chief was being with him. Even though his appearance scared Uko and he openly admitted being the leader of the bad guys, his polite manner didn't seem to match Uko's vision of him.

"What do you mean Detectives have done more harm than good?" Uko asked.

"Greed and self-interest is a scorn of every group. Detectives are not perfect. I have heard of Detectives who have been nothing short of terrors with those who they're supposed to help. I once watched a young Detective botch an assignment with a little girl and then blame the child for the mistake. Who knows how much longer that poor girl continued to have terrible nightmares," Chief replied. He stood up with his cane and began walking to the front of the train.

Uko sat in confusion and continued to stare at the spot where Chief was previously sitting before him.

Chief turned back to Uko and spoke again, "Kids like you are not supposed to know that the world isn't the black and white fairytale we wished it was. It's about winners and losers and there is no honor in losing for the sake of being good. I'm sorry to tell you that," Chief said.

"I think there's a big difference between messing up an assignment as a detective and making people pay you money to learn how to live in a dream. No one's perfect, but you can't use that as an excuse to do whatever you want," Uko said. He rose up and turned to Chief. His voice rose as he spoke, more than he would have imagined in a situation like this. "The rules for a Detective are silly to you because you want to live like an outlaw. I want to do what's right." Chief looked amused at Uko's sudden, assertive display. "If it means stopping people like you from doing whatever you want, then that's what I'll spend my time doing." Uko finished through gritted teeth, released his clenched fists, and look down at his palms surprised at his own reaction. He didn't expect to respond that way.

Chief's bemused look turned to a deep scowl. Uko's brief surge of bravery was quickly zapped and his legs felt rubbery.

"You idiot," Chief said. "I'm literally the light at the end of the tunnel of darkness and ignorance, and here you are rejecting my wise words. Suit yourself."

The train jerked forward again, and the car buzzed back to life. Uko stumbled and caught himself on a handrail. He knew that Chief caused the train to move so he focused his thoughts on stopping it again to prove he had control. Unfortunately, nothing happened. The trained continued to whirl out of the dark tunnel and into a bright afternoon sky.

"We're not in the same league, my friend," Chief stated as he watched Uko struggle. "This may be your dream, but this is my world." As Chief spoke, the train charged into another dark tunnel. The car was lit by the fluorescent bulbs overhead.

"I'm not your peer. Your beloved Detectives fear Coyotes because we can be very bad people. A murderous lot. Who do you think Coyotes fear?" Chief asked. "Me. That's how you control outlaws. By being someone they fear. I can't give you back the time you wasted learning the childish ways of a detective, but I can teach you the freedom of a Coyote."

"I don't need your help," Uko defiantly responded. "I'm happy with the group I have."

"A boy who hasn't even conquered his own self-doubt," Chief said to himself with anger in his voice. "A fool will be a fool. You're not what I expected.

We'll see each other again. But I guarantee when that day happens, you won't be a Nightmare Detective," he added mockingly. "You won't have their support to protect you. You'll have to deal with me all alone. I promise you that," he said. "And at that point you will become my enemy. I'm not kind to my enemies."

"Ok then," Uko said as he tried to control the tremble in his voice. "I'll leave you alone and you leave me alone."

Chief considered his statement and smiled.

"You don't get it do you?" Chief hissed. "I am who I am because I do terrible things to get what I want." He began walking back toward Uko as he spoke. Uko's back was against the train car door.

"A man once owed me something that he refused to pay. I warned him, but he refused again. The nerve. Later that week that man's sweet mother had another one of her routine Pangea dreams. She comes home to a spotless house, food is waiting in the kitchen, and her favorite movie is on the television, paused at her favorite spot; only this time when she entered her home and flicked on her lights, there I was seated at the kitchen table."

Chief stood directly in front of Uko and removed his sunglasses as he finished his story. His cloudy eyes and scarred face were even more frightening up close.

"That woman did not live through that dream. For four more nights I appeared in her kitchen. I'm sure she would tell you that each encounter was worse than the last. Finally, on the fifth day I was paid what was mine. I visited her again to share the great news," Chief said with a smile. "Unfortunately, she burst into tears upon seeing me and we never got a chance to celebrate."

Uko stared at Chief as he spoke, frozen to his spot.

"Those who know the Pangean food chain understand that there is me and only me at the top," Chief said. "Do you understand?"

Uko could not speak. He could only nod his head.

Chief took a step back and put his sunglasses back on with a terrifying smile. "Fantastic."

The train slammed to an abrupt stop. Uko barely braced himself before getting tossed around by the force. The engine and lights shut off again along with the air conditioners. The train sat in complete silence and darkness as Uko stared in the direction where Chief once stood.

In the dark, Uko heard Chief's chilling voice speak to him once more, "Never try to be a hero. Heroes die uncomfortable deaths."

As Chief's final warning ended, the bright lights of the train came back to life. Uko was alone.

***

Uko gasped loudly as he woke up and rose from his bed in his quiet bedroom. His clock told him it was 4AM as he gathered his thoughts. He looked over to his dresser and saw Kanju smiling back at him—childlike, happy, and innocent. Uko got up from bed, picked Kanju up and looked at the tattered lion that he kept as a guardian from bad nightmares. He opened a drawer and put him away. He felt silly for ever depending on a kid's crutch.

Uko returned to his bed and pulled the Survival Scroll notebook from beneath his mattress. He found the flashlight he kept by his bed for nighttime reading and opened the notebook. It was time to study.

CHAPTER 9

Killer Bees in Frankfurt

UKO WOKE UP WITH HIS FLASHLIGHT by his side and his face firmly planted in the Griot's notebook. He thought he may have dozed off for a few minutes while reading, but his clock told him it was a little after noon. As he gathered himself and sat up, he thought about how weird it was that he slept for several hours without remembering any time spent in Pangea. He got up to jot that thought down in his journal when he heard the festive music of Mario Kart loudly playing on the television downstairs. *Femi must be playing the game*, he thought, and he walked down the stairs.

As he entered the basement, he saw Manny, Femi, and Carlos sitting quietly on the couch in front of the TV. Because the game's music played so loudly, they didn't hear or notice Uko as he entered. The boys just sat and stared at the screen as the joyous player selection music played.

"Oh, I didn't know you guys were coming over today," Uko said with giddy excitement. "I know I've been talking about it a lot, but I gotta catch you up on what happened with Toni last night." He stood on the last stair to the basement and waited for a response. No one said anything.

"What's good? No one's talkin'," he said to the group as he crossed the TV and sat on a chair near the end of the couch. "Are you guys gonna start the game or what?"

Femi lifted the remote next to him and lowered the volume a little. Everyone looked more serious than Mario Kart on an early afternoon would require.

"How you doin', man?" Carlos said from his end of the couch. His measured voice and droopy eyes threw Uko off.

"I'm good," Uko responded slowly. He looked around at the other boys who all stared at him with serious interest in his response to this basic question. "Why's everyone acting weird? What happened?"

Carlos looked at Femi who looked down at the remote in his hand.

"You know Derek who got hit by the car yesterday?" Manny asked.

"Yeah."

"He just died in the hospital," Manny said. "Kev just texted Carlos."

"What?" Uko said not wanting to believe the news. He looked at Femi for confirmation. Femi continued to look at the remote. "We saw everything," Uko finally said. "It didn't look that serious. What are you talking about?"

"He hit his head hard on the ground when it happened," Femi said without looking up.

In a flash, Uko could see the entire thing replay itself in front of him. He could see Derek's face up close. He could see the laughter in his eyes as he ran away. He could see the car appear in the driveway behind the bushes. He could hear that deafening screech. The screams of everyone around him were replaced by the sound of the car making impact. Uko shuddered and tried to shake the vision from his thoughts. When his eyes refocused on the room, everyone but Femi was watching him.

"That's..." Uko said before pausing. The grisly replay was coming back, and he had to fight it away. "That's crazy."

"I know," Femi said with anger rising in his voice. "I was cool with his sister before they left our school. They were good people. What happens now? They're just supposed to accept it?"

A nauseous feeling overcame Uko. He placed his hands on his knees to steady himself. Nothing like this had ever happened to anyone around him before and he didn't know what someone was supposed to do in these situations. Femi's comment made Uko think about what he would do if this happened to Femi or their parents. How unfair is it to lose someone that way? He saw Derek's final smile again in his mind and fought the returning nausea. Everyone sat in silence as the video game music continued to cycle through its playlist.

The silence snapped when Femi picked up the remote in his hand and hurled it at the wall across the room. The remote shattered into two pieces, sending batteries and plastic in different directions. The group looked frozen as they stared at the broken remote. After a few moments, Uko stood up. He felt the nausea creep back and he fought it again as he walked over to the spot on the couch next to Femi and sat down. As Femi looked over, Uko saw his puffy, red eyes clearly for the first time. Without saying a word, Uko reached out and hugged his older brother. The other boys watched. "It's ok," Uko said as Femi's fuming died down. The music continued.

***

That evening, Uko gave an extra hug and kiss to his parents before he headed off to bed. After a considerable amount of time spent tossing and turning, he finally closed his eyes and fell asleep. He woke up in the middle of the meadow's dewy grass. The chirps and sounds of nature were familiar and comforting. He caught sight of Toni as she walked up to him. He began cheesing at the thought of going into another dream with her again. Unfortunately, she didn't seem as pleased.

"What the heck took you so long," Toni asked. "I felt like I've been waiting here for months. I thought about building a house since I apparently live here now."

"I'm sorry," Uko replied, "It was tough falling asleep. I had a lot on my mind."

Toni smiled. "You must have been replaying that stupid face you made when you saw Umar's dinosaurs," Toni said as she mimicked Uko's shock from last night.

Uko smiled weakly. Toni continued. "What happened in the dream after? Let me guess, you were at my school and you followed me to my locker and you begged to hang out with me when we're sleep walking. Then I thought about it and I was like 'possibly, but only if you carry my books.'"

"No," Uko said and took a deep breath. "Actually, I saw this kid I used to go to school with get hit by a car yesterday. I found out he died today."

"Are you serious?"

"Yeah."

"And you let me say all those dumb jokes without stopping me?"

Uko shrugged his shoulders.

"Do you want to talk about it?" Toni asked.

"Not really. I think I'd rather just focus on this."

"Ok. If that's what you want," Toni said. Uko looked at her timidly. He was afraid she might judge him for not having an appropriate reaction. But he really didn't know how he was supposed to feel. The only thing he knew for certain was that the entire thing made him feel helpless.

"Did you do any exploring last night after I woke up?" Toni asked.

"Actually, I did," Uko said. "I had a crazy dream in an empty train." Uko filled Toni in on his meeting with Chief and the conversation they had. He was surprised by how strong Toni's reaction was. He knew the meeting was significant, but Toni looked floored. Her jaw dropped, and she stared at him for what felt like an eternity before she finally spoke.

"Chief was in your dream?" she finally asked.

"Yeah. He said he heard about me. He said he watched us when we were in Umar's dream."

Toni blinked and shook her head. "Wait, he was in that kid's dream with us?"

"Yeah. He was a lot creepier that I thought a Coyote would be," Uko said.

Toni did not immediately answer him. Instead she stared at the ground. She started and stopped speaking multiple times as if she couldn't find the right words. Finally, she said, "That was a bad man."

Toni began briskly walking with him toward the Silk Road where they passed into Umar's dream the night before. She spoke quickly but calmly. Uko jogged lightly to keep up with her.

"Chief was a Detective a while ago when he was a kid. People say he was good at it. By the time the monster or the killer or whatever it was came to chase them, the kid was ready to kick into action," Toni said as they walked. "Chief was a beast."

"So, what happened," Uko asked.

"He became obsessed with living in Pangea. His sleep walking life was apparently pretty rough so most of the time he'd sleep all day and travel all over Pangea," Toni said. "I'm piecing the story from what I've heard from different Detectives I've met but I heard when it was time for him to retire, he wouldn't do it. He said it wasn't fair that he had to give up what made him happy and go back to a life that didn't. He felt the other Detectives didn't have the same worries he did while sleep walking."

Uko tried to imagine how a young Detective became the person who threatened him on that train. Was there a misstep along the way or was he just in a bad situation from the beginning?

"That's why I'm so worried about him following us in Umar's dream and him showing up in your dream," Toni continued. "If you've never met someone in Pangea then you would only see them randomly, just like when you're sleep-walking. But if you've met them or you've been introduced to them, then you guys start building a connection to each other. You learn their sleep address. Once that happens, it's much easier to find each other through your DreamHubs. Their dreams start showing up in the fog when you're choosing where you want to jump to in Pangea. It's why I'm able to find you so easily and can meet you in your limbo. Our connection is really strong."

Uko thought about this and realized the unfortunate truth as he spoke it.

"Does that mean he's connected to me now?"

Toni eyes dropped as she replied silently with a slow nod of her head.

Uko felt his heart flutter and rubbed his eyes. Why can't he just have a normal time in Pangea like everyone else?

"I can't catch a break," Uko said as he exhaled deeply. "So, meeting and connecting with people opens up more of Pangea to you; then Chief must be pretty set."

Toni nodded her head again and raised her eyebrows. "I'm sure he is. And he probably won't stop until he can see everyone and everything."

"I feel like we should do more. If kids were able to be Detectives longer and we organized, we would be better and more effective. Plus, we can really start—" Uko said before Toni cut him off.

"Listen Uko. I know you have great ideas and all, but the truth is that there is no 'we' yet. You aren't an official detective. You're still a recruit and you failed your first practice run," Toni said. They were finally at the interior edge of the forest and in complete darkness. They stood side by side, facing the now active purple and gray DreamHub. "You know I have total confidence in you but if you don't pass the final test, you won't be able to join. There aren't any do-overs. I agree that maybe the Detectives can find a way to do more, but there's no way for you to help if you don't make the cut."

Uko was a little hurt at the abruptness of the real talk but he understood why Toni had to say it. He wasn't in yet and until he was, he was just a kid with big ideas.

"Is this nightmare that we're going into my final test?"

"Nope. Thank God because you still suck," Toni said jokingly. "We have one more toddler's nightmare to work in before you take on the final test."

"So, tell me about this one," Uko said.

"No, you gotta find out from the client yourself. Practice what it's like when the bullets are real."

"Will there be bullets," Uko nervously asked.

"Hope not," Toni replied. "I got dressed up for this."

Uko took a deep breath. "I'm ready."

"Well alright. Ladies first," Toni replied as they stepped forward.

***

Toni and Uko appeared, with squinted eyes, under the bright lights of an immense greenhouse. As far as they could see, they were surrounded by row after row of beautiful, brightly colored flowers. Uko was amazed at the intensity of the deep greens and royal blues of their petals. He had never seen flowers like those before, especially not any with petals that rippled with shifting colors.

The pair of them walked down a row of potted plants in search of the client. Uko realized he could appear at any stage in the dream. The first few minutes were spent looking for a person who didn't know they needed to be found. After walking down rows of flowers the length of school hallways, Toni and Uko decided to split up to find the kid. Toni shot down Uko's idea of yelling out 'hello' until they found him or her because it may not be a great time in the nightmare to freak anyone out.

Uko walked down a narrow hall of flowers to his right while Toni split off and took the row behind her. Uko hoped their search would not take long since he wanted to get started saving lives and doing heroic things as soon as possible. Fairly quickly into his walk, his request was answered. A small child in a white beekeeper's uniform rounded the corner into the path in front of him. The tiny beekeeper had a large helmet with a netted screen over its face. The large gloves looked like what a birthday clown would wear. The beekeeper carefully moved flowers from one shelf to another in the row. Uko jogged down the path and approached his client.

"Hello," Uko said as he extended his hand. "My name is Uko. How are you?"

The beekeeper looked at him with the shocked surprise that comes from hearing a voice in a room you thought was empty. Through the netted screen was a little boy with bright blond hair. The boy extended his hand and shook Uko's.

"Hi," he timidly said.

"What's your name?"

"My name is Finn," he replied. He had an accent Uko could not place, but he spoke English.

"Finn? That's a cool name," Uko replied. "What are you doing, Finn?"

"I'm watering the plants." Finn looked nervous as he spoke. Uko noticed this and attempted to calm him as the two spoke.

"Okay, that's nice. Why do you have the bee costume?" Uko asked.

Finn looked around before answering. "So, I don't get stung by the bees."

"Bees," Uko said warily. "Perfect. Just perfect. I thought you might say that," Uko had a very strong fear of bees ever since getting stung by one during a camping trip two summers ago.

At that moment Toni ran around the corner of their pathway and saw them.

"Bees?" She asked as she approached, panting.

"Bees," Uko confirmed.

"Bees aren't that bad," she said.

"I hate bees," Uko replied.

Their client, Finn, looked from Toni to Uko in confusion.

"I'm sorry," Uko said as he noticed the confusion. "This is Toni. Toni, this is Finn." They shook hands.

"When the bees come, does your suit keep them away?" Uko asked.

"Sometimes," Finn replied. "Sometimes they sting me through the suit and it really hurts."

"That's no fun," Toni said.

"No, it makes me cry."

"Yeah, I would cry too," Toni added. "Where do you live, Finn?"

"Europa-Allee 50; 60327 Frankfurt am Main, Germany," Finn recited in a sing-song voice.

"Aww, that's cute. You know your whole address?" Toni asked as she squatted down to eye level with Finn.

Finn grinned brightly and nodded.

"So, tell me more about these flowers," Uko asked, feeling more confident in his ability to chat up a new client. "They look really nice."

Finn turned his head toward Uko to reply but there were no words that came out of his mouth. Instead, Uko heard a muffled thump in the distance. Although he could see Finn's mouth move and his arms wave wildly as he pointed to different flowers, all Uko could hear were periodic thumps that grew more and more frequent. He looked at Toni for confirmation of the weird sound, but she did not notice him trying to get her attention. Instead she was engaged in muted conversation with Finn.

The wall of flowers that surrounded them became transparent. Uko could suddenly see through the lines of previously green stems and multi-colored petals. He could see the large window panes that lined the walls of the greenhouse and separated it from the outside. He could also see that the greenhouse was much larger than he originally thought. Most importantly, Uko could see what was causing the thumping.

Yellow and black striped bees the size of small pigeons were ramming themselves into the glass walls, flying back two or three feet, and then throw themselves into the glass window again. Uko looked above the line of bees at the windows and could see huge swarms of them slicing through the air to join the assault. All the while, he heard the thump, thump, thump continue. As the vision of what lay beyond crystalized for Uko, the flowers regained their original color and his view was again shrouded by the wall of plants around him. He turned to see Finn and Toni staring at him in silence.

"What's wrong?" Finn asked.

"Bees, giant bees," Uko exclaimed, "I think we need to hide."

As the last syllable escaped Uko's lips, a screeching crack erupted throughout the room. Finn screamed as the sound of falling glass echoed around them. Uko crouched as low as he could, covered Finn's mouth, and pulled him under the shelf of flowers beside them.

"Toni, come on!"

Toni ducked her head and crawled underneath the waist-high shelf of Imported Perriwarble Tutu. Uko held a visibly shaken Finn. A deafening buzzing sound screamed from the back of the room as the large bees entered the greenhouse. Massive slabs of glass cracked and tumbled to the ground. The swarm pressed themselves through the slits that the frontline bees created in the glass.

"How did you know the bees were here?" Toni asked.

"I'm not sure exactly. You guys were talking and then I couldn't hear you. All I could hear was the sound of the bees hitting the glass. Then I saw them break through the walls," Uko answered. The two of them spoke in breathless whispers as Finn noiselessly screamed into the palm Uko placed over his mouth.

Toni looked extremely impressed. "The clues presented themselves to you. Wow," she said. "That's so rare."

Uko's focus was on his client.

"Finn, you gotta calm down. We're gonna be alright. I know it's a little scary but we're gonna be Ok," Uko whispered to Finn. "It's like we're playing hide and seek."

"With killer bees," Toni quipped.

"Thanks, Toni."

Uko scanned the area around them. He crawled out from under the shelf and pulled several pots of plants to use as a barricade against the bees. There was a hum of buzzing as the bees zigged and zagged through the air above them.

"Hey, Finn," Uko said, "should we be wearing anything special now that the bees are here?"

Finn looked at Toni and Uko in their casual clothing and back at himself in a full beekeeper uniform and nodded yes. "You need to look like me."

"Very true," Uko said, "So can you put a uniform on us just like you? Close your eyes, really imagine it, and then open your eyes."

Toni smiled as she watched Uko give instruction. Finn complied and shut his eyes tight as he imagined his new friends in beekeeper uniforms like him. When he opened his eyes, Uko and Finn sat next to him in bright pink beekeeper suits.

"Interesting color choice," Uko said as he looked at himself.

"I love it," Toni said. "Now, how do we get rid of the bees?"

"Smoke," Finn replied. His face lit up as an idea came to him and he pushed the plant barricade in front of them aside and rushed out of their hiding place. Uko and Toni hurried out behind him, trying to figure out what Finn had in mind.

"Follow me," Finn said as he dashed toward the back of the greenhouse. The massive bees were in a dizzying frenzy all around them, dipping in and out of their way. Toni, Finn, and Uko kept their heads ducked as they dashed forward.

As Uko caught up to a fully sprinting Finn, he looked up toward the ceiling to get a better look at what was around him. The bees were incredibly fast, but they did not seem to be interested in bothering them. The sight of massive bees flying so close made Uko uneasy. He lost any remaining calm when he turned to look at Toni and saw a bee a few inches from his face on a crash course for her head.

"Ahhh!" Uko yelled as he instinctively swatted the bee away. He felt the weight of the insect against his hand as he hit it clear across two rows of plants.

"No, don't hit them!" Finn screamed. As he spoke, the frantic but peaceful flight of the bees took a turn for the worse. They all faced the group at the same time, flashed their imposing stingers, and swooped in for retaliation. Everyone was immediately hit by two or three bees. Thankfully, their suits warded off any initial damage. But by the eighth or ninth bee, Uko could feel a bee's stinger rip through his suit and pierce his skin. He screamed in pain and fell. Toni turned to help but was distracted when her suit tore from the successive attacks. Finn turned but was frozen in fear.

Uko saw a terrified Finn and ran to him despite his pain and pulled the little boy under another shelf of plants. Toni did the same with a shelf on the opposite side of the aisle. Facing each other, both groups frantically pulled plants together to shield themselves as the bees closed in. Uko was worried about being hurt again, but he kept it together as he spoke.

"We need something to get rid of the bees. I think you said that smoke would do the trick, right?"

Finn slowly nodded his head yes. "Bees calm down when they're in smoke."

"Ok, cool. We should make a smoke gun," Uko added. "Like a smoke cannon or something. Right?"

A group of bees began pushing through the leaves of the plants meant to protect them. Uko swatted them away while remaining focused on Finn.

"Great, so can you make a smoke cannon for me, you, and Toni," Uko asked. "I want a big one. And make it pink like my suit."

Finn laughed and closed his eyes. When he opened them, he saw Uko holding a small bright pink cannon.

"What happened," Uko asked as he stared at what looked like a toy in his hands, "It's so tiny."

Before Finn could speak, a gust of thick gray smoke shot into their hiding place. Toni was on the other side of the aisle, blasting her new toy at every bee in sight. The previously aggressive swarm of bees around them began moving in slow motion as they were covered by Toni's blast.

"Keep spraying," Finn yelled to the group, now with a second wind of courage. Finn picked up his massive smoke gun, which was as big as him, and covered the aisle in thick smoke.

Uko grabbed Finn's hand and pushed through their plant barricade. Toni stood in the center of the aisle as she wafted plumes of smoke in every direction while laughing. Finn began laughing too as he sprayed at each group of bees that arrived in their aisle. Uko joined in, making a thick cloud around them as they weaved down the path.

After a few minutes of this, they made it out of the greenhouse. It was curiously calm and free of bees on the outside. Uko congratulated Finn on guiding them from the greenhouse and Toni congratulated Uko on guiding his client. The entire group exchanged hugs and high fives as the grass and sky around them constantly changed colors.

"The dream gets weird when people are about to wake up," Toni explained. "He'll forget the whole thing once he's up. You did good, Uko. You did good. I think you're ready to hang with the big girls."

CHAPTER 10

Follow the Silk Road

FOR A LITTLE OVER A WEEK after his encounter with Finn, Uko could not have the drama filled sleep that he wanted. He laid down each night, looking forward to seeing Toni in his limbo forest.

Instead, his dreams were a combination of replays of previous times with Toni and thoughts of potential future adventures. At one point he had a dream where the turtles that he and Manny named in the park could talk, and they asked to live in his basement. Overall, it was a week free of dreams, Toni, and all things nightmare detective related. He hated it. Nothing matched Pangea.

After trying everything else, he went to bed on a cool July evening and prayed that Toni would come back.

***

This time he woke up inside the familiar meadow outside the enchanted forest he had grown to love. He was so overcome with excitement that he ran in circles screaming in joy with his hands over his head.

"You look like you won the loser's lottery," a familiar voice said to him from a few feet away.

Uko turned to the voice and immediately ran to the source. "Tonniii," he yelled as he gave her a tight bear hug. "Where have you been all my life?"

"My family went on vacay," Toni said as she pushed him off. "I missed you too."

"I don't get it—did you not sleep while on vacation?" Uko asked.

"You can't explore on your own until you become a detective. I have to be with you for now. But my parents took us to Tokyo. They've always wanted to go," Toni replied. "Tokyo time is twelve hours ahead so when you were sleeping, I was wide awake doing touristy things with my folk."

"Oh ok," Uko said. "Well no more vacations, Toni. You're leaving me here to have regular dreams like a dummy."

Toni laughed, put her arm around his shoulders, and led him towards the forest like old times.

"That last dream with Finn went pretty well. Not perfect, but pretty well for a recruit," Toni said. "You guided your client along the way. You built up his confidence and you let him get out of the situation with his own imagination. When things went crazy, you didn't flip out. I was a little proud."

"Thank you," Uko said. "Only a little proud?"

"Just a little," Toni said. "I don't wanna get you too hyped about a toddler's dream. That's still minor league stuff, even though the bees were ginormous."

"So, what are we doing tonight," Uko asked. "Maybe one more practice round with a kid in

Rome or something since you've been gone so long, and I've gotten rusty?"

"Nope, we're all out of practice rounds," Toni said. "It's time for the real thing; the final test for a young recruit. The big one."

Uko pulled away from Toni. "What?!" He placed his hand on his forehead and began to pace. "I think I should have one more practice round. I barely finished that one with Finn and I failed the one before with Umar. I'm definitely not ready for the real thing." As he said this, the tall grass they walked through on the way to the tree line dampened and began sticking to their legs.

Toni frowned. "You gotta stop doubting yourself. You're ready for this, kid. I believe in you," Toni said glancing down. "What's going on with this grass?"

***

Uko and Toni arrived at the edge of the Silk Road that led them to deep sleep. Uko envisioned this moment a million times in the long week since he last saw Toni. Now that they were here in the nighttime flesh, Uko was terrified. He hoped that this would be another low pressure run around the practice track. Instead, he was being thrown into a win/lose test to determine whether he could join the squad.

"Who will the client be?" he asked.

"It'll probably be someone closer to your age. Sometimes they're a little older. Other times they're a little younger. But it'll be close," Toni replied.

"So, I have to do the same thing I did with Finn?"

"Yeah, but better this time."

"Ok, ok," Uko said as he took deep breaths and nodded his head vigorously. "What was the scariest nightmare you've ever been in?"

Toni looked to the sky and thought about the question for a moment. "There's been so many that you kind of blend them together after a while," she said. "I remember one client where we were trapped in their school and there was someone with a gun. That was scary because it felt so real. I had to keep reminding myself that we wouldn't really die. I hated that one, but I ended up helping them get out safely. I woke up that morning and cried. There are so many terrifying things that happen in everyday life that people take with them to bed."

The two of them stood in silence after Toni spoke. Uko imagined how he would have done in the same situation and things did not turn out well.

"Would getting shot feel as painful as it would in real life?" Uko asked.

Toni didn't immediately answer. "It would feel as painful as your mind thinks a gunshot would be."

"Your brain is what tells you that your body is in pain. If a nightmare seems real enough to your brain, it'll think that you've been hurt," Toni added. "The more time you spend in people's nightmares, especially really bad ones, the harder it is for your mind to tell the difference between real and fake."

"So that's why we're not supposed to be a detective for our whole lives," Uko said.

"Yeah," Toni said. "That's probably one of the biggest reasons."

Uko took a deep breath and stopped pacing. "Whelp, let's go in." He held out his hand, Toni grabbed it, and they stepped onto the Silk Road before them.

Uko walked slower than normal down the darkening path with Toni. He did his best not to overthink the upcoming challenge, but it was hard for him not to have cold feet. The little success he had before would now be put to a test he felt he would likely fail. So, in the few moments before entering that final stage, he decided to ask Toni every question that crossed his mind since meeting her. At least he would have one last nice conversation before returning to his normal sleep walking life.

He opened his mouth to begin, but Toni beat him to it. "There's a reason I helped you in three separate nightmares before I asked you to join the squad," she said. "Every detective has to find their replacement, but the ultimate goal is finding someone even better than you ever were. If you can do that when you retire, the Detectives will be in even better hands than when you started. So when I first met you and I saw you in action, I had this feeling that you were going to be the one to come in and be better than I ever was."

Uko was flattered by the comment and didn't know how to respond.

"That's nice of you to say."

"Nice?"

"I mean, thanks." Uko pinched his leg in frustration. *Get it together!* "I'm saying. You keep tellin' me stuff like that, but what did I do that was so great?"

"You improvised. Whenever an obstacle popped up, you would think of a way around it. It was like you were having fun coming up with plans C and D and E. Everyone looks great when things go the way you expect them too. Life is about adapting when things don't," Toni said.

Although it was increasingly darker as the two of them sauntered down the path, Uko looked in Toni's direction as she spoke. He wanted to use this time wisely. If Toni was in such a compliment-giving mood, maybe this would be a good time for him to share his own for her.

"After the second or third nightmare with you, I knew I was right," Toni continued. "I was so glad that I found a successor who would be so top-of-the-class that I would even tell other clients about you. I knew they would forget our conversation when they woke up, but I had to tell someone." Toni laughed at the memory.

"Can I tell you something?" Uko asked.

"Sure."

"This is the best summer I've ever had. Ever. It's not even close. I think about being a detective all day. I daydream and wish I was asleep, so I can come back here," Uko said. He blushed at the thought that he might be coming off too strong. Sure, he loved coming to Pangea, who wouldn't? But what made this such an incredible time was Toni and Toni specifically. He was now realizing this clearly—even if he couldn't bring himself to say it with that same clarity. "I'm really glad you saw something in me. You're one of the best dream mentors ever. Top 3 definitely."

"Oh, only one of the best," Toni said. "Because you've had so many mentors."

"Yeah, I didn't tell you? I had another guy a couple months ago teach me about this nightmare thing, but I was busy back then, so they had to stick me with you," Uko said. "They called it community service before I joined the force."

"Oh, is that so? I'm community service for the kid scared of cut out dinosaurs," Toni replied. As she spoke, her voice cracked slightly and the words muddled together. She cleared her throat before speaking again but it didn't help. Uko heard her sniffle loudly.

"Are you Ok," Uko asked.

"Yup," she whispered. "Perfectly fine."

Now that they were entering the darkest part of the forest, they could not see each other's faces. They were back to relying on Uko's intuition for which direction to walk as he guided them over unseen rocks and logs.

"What are you like when you're not fighting nightmares?" Uko asked. "What's your life like?"

"I'm just a regular girl. I've got a younger brother and an older sister. I just got a puppy named Hercules that I love," Toni said. "And this summer my best friend's gonna show me how to play chess."

"Do you have a lot of friends?" Uko asked.

"Yeah I guess so. What about you?"

"No, not really. A couple."

"That's fine," Toni said. "They're overrated anyway."

"I doubt it," Uko said. He decided it was best to steer the conversation away from his lonely personal life. "I remember when you were with me against The Skeleton King. You said something about us being the same person or something. Were you saying that I created him?"

"Kind of. The Skeleton King is your self-doubt that's come to life. Everyone has a part of them like that. With the imagination of a detective, that nasty part of us takes a creepy form and haunts us whenever it can and all we can do is fight it. Mine is an old lady with one eye and long gray hair."

"Can we destroy it?"

"No."

Uko took this in. "Can it destroy us?"

"Yes."

As Toni spoke, the pair reached the end of the path. In total darkness they stared forward at the pathway to Uko's destiny. Toni turned toward Uko and took both of his hands into hers.

"Let's stop for a second," Toni said. "I want to tell you something important."

Uko stopped and looked toward Toni. He hoped she might be taking this moment to tell him that she shared the same feelings he had about her.

"This is the last time you and I will walk through this forest together," Toni began. "If you make it, you'll become an official detective and I won't be able to guide you through anymore nightmares. After the test tonight, we'd meet in another dream and I would go through the final instructions on how to get in and out of dreams and how to be a great Detective for other kids. Then, I officially retire and go back to boring ol' Sleep Walking life in Savannah."

Uko began breathing slowly to control the worry he was feeling. He figured Toni had something important to say but he didn't expect it to be final goodbyes.

"If you don't make it through the test, if your client doesn't solve the nightmare on their own," Toni continued, "then you'll wake up and forget any of this ever happened. You go back to being the kid you were before you met me. And yes, that means that you'll forget about me."

"I don't want to go back," Uko finally said. "And I don't want you to retire. We're a good team, why can't we just keep doing this together?"

"You know we can't. Besides, you'd probably just slow me down anyway," Toni responded. "You're gonna be great without me. Even after I retire, I'm gonna remember you as one of my favorite recruits and think about how you made me so proud."

"One of your favorites?"

"Top 3 definitely."

Uko felt drips of water fall onto his hands. Even though he could not see a single thing in front of him, he was sure those drips were tears. He looked into the abyss at where his hands would be and thanked God for the dark that covered his own tears.

"As long as you don't tell people it was community service," Uko said.

Toni both laughed and sniffled. "No never that."

"I like you," Uko said to his surprise.

"I like you too, you're cool," Toni replied.

Uko bit his lip at the reply. He figured she didn't understand what he meant, but he couldn't repeat himself. He had already used all his effort to say it the first time.

"Are you ready for this?" she asked.

"No" he said.

"Me neither."

Uko chuckled to keep from shedding more unseen tears. They stepped forward and the DreamHub's thick, colorful fog began dripping from the sky before them. It quietly crawled over their feet.

"Well at least none of us are prepared. That always works," he said.

"Yeah," Toni said quietly as the two stepped forward. "It always does."

CHAPTER 11

Deserted City

BRIGHT STREAMS OF LIGHT shone on Uko's face, making it difficult to take in his surroundings. He immediately noticed that his neck and arm were stinging with pain, as though he'd fallen asleep in an awkward position. He realized that instead of standing in an open space like he did when entering the practice nightmares of Finn and Umar, Uko was compressed in the back of a small car that had clearly been in a terrible accident. He gasped and felt a sinking feeling in his belly at the realization. The effort to free himself was draining and he had to awkwardly twist to slide his right arm out from the wreckage. The cracked window in the passenger door beside him revealed the hood of a mangled white van that had slammed into Uko's vehicle moments before.

"Toni," he whispered to no response. He hated the anxiety this was already causing in him. He cautiously sat up to see what he could find in the car that might lead him to Toni. The passenger seat in front of him was littered with chunks of glass, scattered papers, and torn books. As he turned his head to survey the driver seat, the only thing he noticed was the pair of bloodshot eyes that looked back at him.

Before Uko's brain could process that the eyes belonged to an angry looking man covered in dirt and sweat, the man reached out and grabbed him. He grasped Uko's shirt and pulled. Uko screamed for help. As the anxiety morphed into full blown terror, Uko ripped at the hand with all his might. The effort didn't help. The man was much stronger than him and he nearly pulled Uko's entire body into the front seat.

Uko stopped focusing his effort of freeing himself from the man's grip. Instead he used his free hands and legs to keep himself in the rear of the car and as far away as possible. Thick beads of sweat dripped from his head as he struggled. As Uko attempted to push away from the attacker, a thought flashed into his mind. Before he could process it and decide whether it was a good idea, the entire car jerked backward as another car slammed into them from the front. The man's grip was immediately released and Uko was thrown into the corner of the rear seat as an incredibly loud crunch shot through the car. He stared at the roof motionless for a few seconds of shock. The same terrible screeching sound he heard when he witnessed Derek being hit by a car a few days ago came back in full force. It reverberated in his head and drowned out everything around him. Uko covered his ears to block it out, but it didn't work.

"Are you alright?" Toni screamed to Uko from some distance outside of the wreckage.

"No," Uko screamed back as he shakily sat up and struggled to open the door next to him. "I appeared in here and this guy just attacked me out of nowhere. Then I had a weird idea about a car hitting us and the next thing I know, we got hit by a car."

"Uko, you don't have to scream. I'm right here. And what guy," Toni asked as she stepped up to the car and looked inside to see Uko, debris and nothing else.

Uko pulled himself forward to look into the driver seat. The screech still rang in his head and caused him to squint but Toni seemed unaffected. As he looked around, he saw that there was nothing there but more glass and an ejected airbag.

"There was a guy here seconds ago," Uko said to Toni. "He was grabbing my shirt and I tried to get away. What happened?"

"He probably got erased," Toni said as she looked for a way to help Uko out of the car. "This nightmare that we're in is really unstable. The client's mind is adding and getting rid of stuff as they go along. I saw some people when I first got here, and they disappeared after a few seconds."

"Why is that happening?" Uko asked.

"It could be different reasons. The client might be having a hard time staying asleep so they're tossing and turning."

Uko thought about that as he crawled through the busted window in the door next to him. Toni checked him to see if he was seriously hurt, but he was only just a little bruised. The car that slammed into Uko while he was being attacked was still lodged into the front of the vehicle they stood next to. Smoke billowed out of the hood and wafted through the street. They noticed that although they were in the middle of a wide and busy street, there was no movement around them. Cars were abandoned up and down the block. Some had their doors open, some were pulled off to the side of the road, and some were abandoned right in the middle of the street. In addition to this desertion, Uko and Toni noticed the incredible silence. There were no birds chirping, people talking, or leaves rustling. Even though it looked like they were in a crowded city, they didn't hear any sounds besides their own.

"We have to find the client quickly before they wake up. It doesn't matter what wakes them up. If you don't help them solve the nightmare before they do, you lose," Toni said.

"Well, then let's go," he said. They chose a random direction and began jogging down the block.

Nothing around Uko and Toni remained calm while they jogged. Mailboxes and trees zapped in and out of view. The edges of cars and buildings zigged and zagged like images on a television with poor reception. With every peculiar instance of the flickering, Toni seemed to become more and more worried. The sight of her anxious face, more than anything else, sent Uko's heart rate soaring through the roof.

As they rounded the corner onto a smaller block, Uko heard the first sound since exiting the car. He could not make out any words, but he was certain he heard faint screams.

"Do you hear that?" he asked Toni.

"No, hear what?"

"I think I hear someone screaming for help," he replied before sprinting in the sound's direction.

"Wait for me," Toni said as she followed.

Uko eventually stopped in front of a short, brick building that had an old, wooden porch. As Toni caught up to him, she could hear the screaming for the first time. It came from an open window on the top floor.

"Stay away from me," the voice yelled. "Stay away!"

"I think that's the client," Toni said. Uko was already on the porch, lunging for the door. He opened it and waved for Toni to join him as he hurried up the rickety stairs that led to the top of the building.

After running up several flights of stairs, they reached a floor at the top with three closed doors. Uko panted with exhaustion as he asked Toni which door she thought the sound came from. Toni shrugged, so they pressed their ears to each one in hopes of hearing another signal. Unfortunately, no sound came from either door.

"Let's just go in each one," Uko said.

"Okay, you first," she responded.

Uko placed his hand on the handle of the door closest to him and opened it. He saw the old brick of the house next to the building they were in. Strangely, the door that Uko opened led directly outside. He briefly looked down to see they were several stories up. He stepped back, shut the door, and turned to Toni.

"Let's try your door."

As quietly as possible she opened her door only to see a tiny, empty closet. "Nothing," she said and turned back to Uko. His hand was already placed on the handle of the third and final door.

"Let's open it together," he said.

Toni placed her hand over Uko's as they braced themselves. Although the hallway they stood in was completely silent moments before, once the door opened, they were overwhelmed with the sounds of a struggle. Toni and Uko froze in shock at the sight of five large men and an even larger woman in front of them. The group wore dirty, mismatched clothing. They didn't notice Uko and Toni's entrance because all their focus was on a girl who stood a few feet in front of them. They slowly approached her while she screamed for help.

Uko was also caught off guard by the sight of the adults in tattered clothing. But what truly stunned him was the girl screaming for help.

The girl that the adults seemed intent on capturing was Imani Gimble: the cute, basketball star, cool girl that Uko once thought might be interested in him until The Council convinced him otherwise. Of all the people he could go down swinging with in his final test to become a detective, it had to be Imani. Great. Even in this stressful situation, she looked incredible.

Toni tugged on Uko's shirt to try and quietly signal him to follow her. There was an open room immediately to their right and Toni wanted to duck into it and regroup while they were still unseen. Uko would not respond. He was still overcoming the surprise of seeing someone he knew. Toni tugged harder but Uko would not move. Before Toni could try another and more aggressive attempt, Imani caught sight of the two of them.

"Uko?!"

The adults who were once facing Imani turned toward Uko and Toni. For a split second, everyone just stared as the entire room was surprised to see each other.

Finally, one of the men in the group spoke.

"Get them!" he shouted, and the rest ran toward Uko and Toni.

Suddenly, gray walls rose up in random spots between Uko and Imani's group. They noisily cracked the floor around them and sprung up like a flower growing in warp speed. Even though Uko and Toni's vision of their pursuers was momentarily blocked, they could get a better view if they stood on their toes. The gray barriers were only a few feet tall so a short hop or an outstretched neck could help them see over two or three walls. The result was a maze of gray walls that suddenly separated everyone in the room and provided a few moments for Uko and Toni to figure out a plan.

"Find them," a voice from across the sea of maze walls yelled out. A stampede of feet followed and Uko could see the head of one of the men as he began climbing over walls.

"Keep your head down and follow me," Toni said as she ducked and charged into the maze. Uko always appreciated how she seemed to know what to do regardless of the situation.

Uko ran in behind her, keeping his eyes on Toni as she darted around corners. The walls shook with the storm of Toni and Uko looking for Imani while the strangers looked for them. Eventually they both entered a stretch of walls that created a tight hallway within the room. At the end of the path, they saw Imani looking around as she crouched. Toni darted toward her while Uko followed. His heart skipped a beat as they closed in. Nightmare or not, he was seconds away from the moment of truth.

"Uko what are you doing here?" Imani said a little too loudly when the two approached. Her voice was shrill and nasally. Did it always sound like that?

"Shhh," Toni responded. "Uko and I are here to help you. You're in a nightmare right now."

"I'm in a what?" Imani asked, even louder.

 175

"Can you keep your voice down? Please," Toni replied with frustration.

"Ok," Imani said at the same volume. Uko cocked his head to the side as he looked at her. Was it just him or was she completely oblivious to the danger that was going on around them?

"Hey Imani," Uko said as smoothly as he could.

"Hey," she replied unenthusiastically.

Uko looked at Toni while thinking of something to say next. She looked back and mouthed "Talk!"

"Are you alright?" he finally asked.

"Yeah," she replied and left it at that. Uko knew he was a little nervous, but Imani didn't make conversation easy. Toni rolled her eyes and shook her head.

As Toni turned to see if any of the men made it to their area, Uko noticed a shadow cover her feet. He looked up to see what caused the shadow and was greeted by the stained smile of a burly man in an oversized sweatshirt. He perched above the wall a few feet from them and pointed in their direction when he noticed the group.

"They're over here," he yelled.

Toni grabbed Imani's hand and dashed down the path between the walls toward a door at the end of the room. Just as they reached the door, it swung open and the woman that Uko saw earlier emerged. She playfully twisted her finger in her matted and frayed hair as she stepped into the room. She blocked their only escape.

"Get ready to jump!" Uko yelled from behind the group. He was more comfortable now that they were on the move again and had an idea.

"What?" Toni yelled back in confusion.

As Toni turned to Uko to understand what he meant, a massive hole opened under the feet of the woman who walked toward them. With a loud crash, she fell through the hole and out of their vision.

"Jump," Uko said as he pointed to the gap that was now between them and the door.

Toni and Imani didn't break stride and leaped toward the open door. They both landed gracefully past the threshold and turned with outstretched arms to Uko. Uko attempted his jump but slipped while taking off. He barely made it across the hole before falling and grabbing Imani's arm to keep him from going down. Toni had to grab Imani and pull her back to make sure she didn't fall in the hole with Uko. Uko used his free arm to pull himself up while Toni pulled him into their room. Toni and

Uko collapsed in exhaustion. Imani pulled back and looked down at the fingernails on her left hand.

"Damn, Uko! You broke my nail," Imani shouted. Toni and Uko chuckled, thinking that Imani was kidding given all that they went through. She wasn't. "What's happening anyway," Imani angrily asked no one in particular. "What is all of this?"

Uko did his best to ignore her attitude and do his job.

"You're in a nightmare that my friend Toni and I are here to help you get out of here safely," Uko said. "Except I think we made it worse because now we're being chased by Coyotes."

"That's the last time you can do something that drastic on your own Uko," Toni chimed in. "I mean the hole out of nowhere trick was pretty impressive, but you won't pass if you do too much by yourself."

Uko blushed as he replied, forgetting Imani was there. "I'm just glad it worked. It's not like we got a lot of time to talk things out."

"You're right," Toni said. "Go right ahead and explain." She put her hand outward and did a mock bow.

"Ok," Uko started as he turned back to Imani. "So, I know it sounds really weird but–"

"Are you and your little girlfriend gonna help me find my brother or what," Imani interrupted.

Uko jerked his head back and looked to Toni. "Oh, um.... no. She's not my girlfriend. I mean, that's not to say. I mean," he said before pausing and looking at his shoes.

"Well done, Uko," Toni remarked. "Let's keep moving."

***

Back outside, the group walked down a desolate block. Uko tried to explain what he and Toni were doing there. He stumbled through a painfully drawn out explanation of detectives and Coyotes that Imani went along with to get him to stop talking. The world around them continued to act strangely as old newspapers randomly blew past them and transformed into tumbleweeds before abruptly disappearing. As they walked, the sky would turn bright blue, gray with clouds, dark with stars, and rain within the span of a few minutes. Imani's mind continued to mix and match ideas on a whim.

"Why were those guys chasing you?" Toni asked.

"I don't know. I was walking through the park with my brother and they came out of nowhere and tried to take us away," Imani said. "They took my brother, but I was able to run to this building before they got me. One guy was chasing me in a car, but he crashed into another car, so I got away."

While she spoke, Uko tried to decide whether he was lucky or unlucky to get her as his final test client. She was just as beautiful as he remembered from school. But being around her now introduced Uko to her personality. She didn't get Uko and Toni's jokes and she didn't seem interested when Toni tried to get to know her. Uko decided he'd be better off just focusing on getting through the dream and passing his final test.

"I can help you find your brother," Uko said as they wandered through the empty streets.

"How?" Imani asked.

"Look up there." Toni pointed up the road to where a crowd of people gathered around a large fire in the street. Toni and the group ducked behind one of the many abandoned cars and tried to devise a plan.

"Who are those people?" Imani asked.

"It's a combination. Some of them you created in your dream. They're the people who kidnapped your brother. The others are the Coyotes. They're the people who tried to grab you in that building. They followed us into this nightmare," Toni responded. "That makes things a lot more difficult, but it's not impossible."

"Tell us about your brother," Uko asked. He was always a better listener than speaker and in moments like these, he realized he should lean on that skill to help solve the case.

"Okay. He's my younger brother. He's ten. He goes to a different school than us. His name is Marcus," Imani said. "He was wearing a blue and white sweater. He just got a cell phone, so he was playing with it when the guys came."

As Uko listened and tried to come up with a plan, the world around them continued to flicker in and out of focus. The size of the group around the fire ahead of them swelled and shrank between 15 and 50 as people vanished and were replaced haphazardly. Toni turned to Uko to speak but she lost her words as she saw the new member of their group crouching behind the car beside them. Toni stared at him in shock with her mouth open.

"What is it," Uko asked. Toni could do nothing but point behind Uko.

Both Imani and Uko turned to see a man in old and torn clothing. After appearing out of thin air, the man stared at them menacingly in silence.

Uko pulled back and covered his mouth to suppress a scream that rushed out. Toni let out a loud scream and tried to crawl away from the man. Uko tried to quiet her down but it was too late. The loud noises got the attention of the group they were hiding from. As Imani, Toni, and Uko ran away from their surprise visitor, every head turned toward them. What was once a group of around 50 people when they were hiding was now a huge crowd of more than 100 creepy men and women.

"Get them!" a voice in the crowd yelled out as they began chasing the kids.

Uko and the group ducked through an alley between two buildings that separated the block with the crowd from the next block. They ran into the open door of one of the buildings and entered a warehouse filled with abandoned forklifts and heavy packages. After they entered, they ran toward the back without knowing where safety was. Eventually, they arrived at a small, unlit office room.

"Uko!" Toni yelled as she stared at her hands. Her entire body was flickering intensely like so many other things they've seen in the nightmare. "I'm fading out. I'm getting kicked from the nightmare." She looked up at Uko with impossibly wide eyes and tears on her cheeks. He had never seen the cool, calm, and collected Toni so terrified. For a moment that seemed like an eternity frozen in time, the sight overwhelmed him.

"What? Why?" Uko asked. "What's going to happen?"

"Imani's going to wake up soon," she said with a frantic tone in her voice. "No! You can't lose this."

Seeing Toni so worried strengthened Uko's resolve. It felt like a surge of electricity passed through him. "It's ok," he said. "I got this."

Toni looked from her flickering hands to Uko's face. The anguish in her face gave way to slight confusion.

"You gave me all I need," Uko said. His voice was firm and authoritative. He infused the next sentence with sweetness and caring. "I'll see you soon." He reached out to reassuringly hold Toni's hand one last time, but it was too late. Toni flickered and completely vanished before their hands touched. In the blink of an eye it was as if she was never there. Uko was left to stare at the spot his mentor once stood. It was his final test and it was down to him and a girl he was growing tired of.

CHAPTER 12

Hope Has Died

"WHAT HAPPENED? UKO WHAT HAPPENED?! Where did she go?" Imani asked in a partial scream.

Uko could not respond.

"Did they take her too? Is that what happened to my brother?" Imani said before falling to the ground and weeping.

Uko was fighting his own battle. He always felt out of his league with the nightmare detective tests, but this took the cake. He had no do-overs, no mentor, and no idea how he would succeed. He sat down next to a crying Imani and a tear rolled down his own cheek. He tried his best, but this was it. Soon the nightmare would be over, and his opportunity would vanish with it. He felt sick at the thought of how unfair it all was. He had the determination to figure out a solution but had no idea what that could be.

As he raked his mind for ideas puddles of water slowly sprang up in random spots. Thick beads of salty water dripped down the walls, as if they cried along with Imani. Eventually, the feeling of kneeling in water caught Uko's attention. He looked down at his hands and knees and saw they were submerged.

"Why is it raining in here?" Imani said between sobs.

Her question was answered with a growl. It was the growl of a voice that Uko recognized as soon as it uttered its first syllable. He partly knew it had to come to this and hearing the voice gave him strength. He rose up rod straight, as though his spine were made of steel.

"My dear boy! Oh, how I've missed you!"

Imani screeched at the jolt of hearing another voice. She noticed the water that surrounded them, stood up, and looked to Uko.

"What's happening?"

"He's here for me," Uko replied solemnly.

"Who's here?"

"The Skeleton King."

As Uko said this, they heard the once empty warehouse filling with the sounds of storming feet. Uko did not need to be told that this was the Reaper army of nightmares past. In his weakest moment, they were here to collect. This time, the eerie sounds of their charging hollow feet were accompanied with voices of men and women.

"We searched the other doors, they have to be in here," one of the women said.

"It's those people again. The Coyotes," Imani whispered as they heard the voice.

The crowd that they ran from with Toni was now filling the building. Uko and Imani looked into the warehouse through a small window in the office they hid in. They saw Reapers, Coyotes and mysterious men and women filling the warehouse in rapid succession. As they entered, they fanned out in different directions, being sure to cover all exits and hope of escape. Eventually, the Reapers entered the warehouse and stepped to his right to make way for a final entrant. The Skeleton King strode in with his head held high. With his large staff at his side and his ragged cloak flaring in the wind, he instantly looked to Uko. The King pulled back the hood of his cloak and revealed his familiar lipless grin.

"Surely you are not surprised. This was how it was destined to end. You were playing on a field above your level," the King hissed. "We're here to grant you mercy and remove you from the game."

Imani backed away from the window that separated them from the intruders.

Uko turned to her. "Don't be afraid. This is a nightmare and those things are a part of it. But I'm not gonna let them hurt us. Okay?"

Imani nodded. Uko tried to think of what Toni would do in a situation like this. How she would take charge without a second thought.

"We need to get rid of this window to protect ourselves," Uko said. Imani did not respond.

"Remember, this is your nightmare. Use your imagination and get rid of this window. What would you use to cover it?" he continued.

Uko turned back to the large window and it quickly shrunk until it was replaced with the wooden wall that originally framed it. They now stood in a room that was slowly filling water that was completely closed off from the skeleton army and Imani's pursuers.

"Perfect. Because this is a nightmare, we can do whatever we want," Uko quickly said. "Imani, if you think about it, you can make it happen. Does that make sense?"

Imani shook her head.

"Visualize it. Think about it happening. I know this is a lot all at once, but I'm here to help you," Uko said. As he spoke, the wall, where the window once was shook with a heavy pounding. The forces outside were fighting their way in. "Get rid of the water in this room. Don't worry about anything else."

"I don't know how," Imani said in distress.

"Visualize it. The water dripped down the walls when you were crying—imagine it going in the opposite direction. Just focus on that, nothing else."

Imani closed her eyes and the water immediately began to recede. There was a loud slurping sound, like water being sucked into a drain, as it crawled back up the walls and left the room. When she opened her eyes, the floor and walls were again dry.

"I did it!"

Uko clapped his hands and laughed. "Yes, you did! Now let's—"

A clawed hand broke through their protective wall. The bone grip of a skeleton grabbed a chunk of the wall and pulled it out. A Reaper's face appeared in the hole before retreating and ripping it open wider with its hand. It repeated this as more hands bore holes into different parts of the wall. Uko could hear the angry voices of people as they barked orders to each other in their attempt to enter the room. He picked up a piece of the broken wall and tried to hit the hands as they shot through. It didn't seem to be working.

"Let's get out through here," Imani screamed to Uko from the back corner of the room. She stood over a large trap door that she held open while waving him to her. Apparently, while Uko was busy fighting the hands, Imani was in the back opening an escape hatch. Uko was amazed.

"Did you make that?" he asked pleased with how quickly she was catching on.

"Just come on," Imani replied.

Uko ran to the door and ducked his head as he went down the stairs into the dark room below.

The complete darkness of the room was the first thing the two of them noticed as the trap door closed above them. After a moment, a torch cracked to life in Uko's hand. As he looked to Imani to instruct her on how to make her own, a second torch illuminated the room from her hand.

"You're a fast learner," Uko said.

"Yeah, I guess so," Imani replied. She was much more cooperative now.

Makes sense. We just need to be on the verge of death and she's a great person to be around, Uko thought.

The pair looked around. They were in the basement of the warehouse, surrounded by large wooden boxes of varying sizes. While they tried to figure out where to go next, the basement filled with light. The trap door they came from was once again opened. Uko and Imani turned to the door to see The Skeleton King standing above the entrance.

"Dear boy, do not crawl around in the dark," the King said. "You need light."

He opened his steely palm and bright red and orange ropes of fire spilled from his hand into the room like flowing water. The fire danced down the stairs before forming balls on the basement floor. The room became incredibly hot as the wooden boxes began igniting with the growing flames.

"We need another door to get out!" Uko scanned the room. Imani picked up an empty wooden box and approached one of the balls of fire on the floor. She used the box to scoop it up and immediately hurled it up at the Skeleton King. The King screamed as the flames quickly engulfed him. He released the trap door and it slammed closed again. The room was once again lit only by the growing flames within.

"Whoa, nice one!" Uko said. Imani smiled back at him.

Uko scanned the room and noticed something odd. All but one of the basement walls were made of solid cinder blocks. On the far end, one wall was simply dirt. He ran to it and began clawing at the dirt with his hands as he tried to burrow a hole. Imani immediately came beside him and dug at the wall with a shovel. Uko smiled to himself, stepped back, and created his own shovel. They both took turns hacking at the wall, carving out a hole while the fire behind them burned. Eventually, light shot into the room from the end of the hole they created.

"This is the way out," Uko said.

"Yeah, let's dig faster," Imani replied.

Covered in sweat from the heat and effort, they broke open a hole big enough for one person to crawl through.

"Go," Uko instructed. "I'll follow."

Imani squeezed through the tight gap and emerged on the other side in an empty room. She turned back and put her hand out to Uko. He grabbed her hand and tried to pull himself through with all his might. Imani used both hands and all her strength to try and yank Uko out. The fire inside the basement raged and was at Uko's feet as he struggled forward. Uko ducked his head and finally rammed through, but the fire claimed his right shoe-melting the laces and a chunk of the sole for good measure.

"Are you ok?" Imani asked, surveying Uko for burns.

"I'm fine," Uko said coolly as he took off his torched shoe. On the inside, he wanted to scream. His shoe had practically burned off!

The bright room that they found themselves in had nothing but stairs that led up to a door. The fire they narrowly escaped continued to consume the basement beside them. Licks of flame turned to fiery hands that swiped and grabbed for them through the gap. Uko stood up and they ran up the stairs to the door. When they reached the top, Uko turned to Imani.

"Here we go," Uko said as he slowly opened the door.

Even though Uko attempted to quietly open the door, it was yanked open from the other side. To their horror and surprise, the Skeleton King stood directly in front of them. His cloak was reduced to strips of cloth that were covered in thick black smoke as they continued to burn, while an army of Reapers stood behind him.

"Hello, friends," he said as he quickly grabbed Uko's shoulder.

That piercing pain Uko felt when a Reaper touched him in his own nightmare was there again in all its glory. He screamed out and tried to free himself but couldn't.

"Run," he told Imani.

Imani did not. Instead she tried to pull The Skeleton King away from Uko with little success. "Seize her!" The Skeleton King yelled, and three Reapers now appeared behind him. They grabbed her arms as the King pulled Uko up toward him.

"This is the end!" The Skeleton King yelled at Uko as their faces met. "You are mine." The bright licks of flames in the Skeleton King's eyes danced in the small space between them. Uko squinted as the Skeleton King's face flashed and flickered intensely before everything went completely dark and all sounds stopped.

***

Out of nowhere, Uko heard Imani screaming. With the scream, light and objects came back into view as well. It was as if everything was being turned on again after a momentary blackout. Uko looked around and saw they were both sitting in chairs facing each other in the center of a dark room. Encircling them were disheveled Coyotes as well as Reapers of different sizes. Everyone held weapons in their hands ranging from bats and sticks to long blades. As Uko looked at Imani, flickered the same way Toni did before she vanished. Everything around Uko flickered and zapped in and out of vision as the Skeleton King's voice pierced the air.

"It's over, dear boy," he said. "Your friend will awaken soon, and this will all end. You will fail just as you were destined. Your effort will be for nothing," the King said as the flickering intensified. "No Nightmare Detectives for you."

Uko did his best to ignore the shouting voice inside that begged him to give up. He scanned the room, looking for a clue that could help him. It felt impossible because everything around him changed so often. In one moment they were in complete darkness, with just the sound of their captors reminding them that they weren't alone. In the next moment, lights flashed on and Uko could see at least three dozen Reapers and Coyotes in every nook and cranny of the dungeon like room. Every attempt to find something unusual, as Toni had explained he needed to do, was a waste of time. Nothing made sense.

"Is everything changing around for you too?" Uko finally said to Imani. The Skeleton King and the captors around him laughed at their prisoner's pathetic question. They looked on as Imani and Uko tried their best to communicate.

"Yes," Imani replied.

"Of course, it is, you fool," The Skeleton King interrupted, "She's waking up."

"I'm trying to keep dreaming," Imani said to Uko in response. "I don't remember what was in this room."

The room was indeed shifting constantly as they sat. Even the walls around them pressed in closer from time to time before retreating to their original locations. An idea came to Uko.

"So, are you changing things around," he asked Imani. "Are you changing everything yourself?"

Imani looked at him confused. "I guess. I'm trying to keep dreaming but it's hard," she replied. She continued to flicker when she spoke. For a moment, she disappeared and reappeared standing and untied. The next moment her hands were tied again to the legs of her chair.

"You have control," Uko shouted excitedly. "You're awake enough to think about what happens next."

The Reapers and Coyotes in the room immediately stopped laughing.

"What does that mean?" Imani asked.

"It means you can get us out. Any way you want," Uko replied.

"No," a voice from the back of the room yelled. The room flashed brighter and everything was bathed in a blinding light. Uko turned to see who spoke but could only make out the outline of a tall man.

The room immediately became pitch black before Uko could see the figure more clearly.

"Get them now, you idiots," the same voice commanded. "He must NOT PASS!"

"Quick!" Uko yelled out to Imani.

The room flashed brightly again, but this time it was filled with the same crates that caught fire in the room that Uko and Imani escaped from earlier. Imani was again untied and standing in front of Uko. The group of Coyotes and Reapers quickly began closing in. Imani took a moment to see the boxes in the room before turning to Uko and smiling.

"Boom," she whispered with a slight smile.

Immediately each crate erupted in flames. Large licks of orange and red fire rose from them and crawled up the walls of the room. The fire started on one side and danced down the line of boxes along the walls. As it reached new sections, some crates would explode and multiply the size of the blaze. The group of Coyotes and Reapers who were once rushing to seize Uko and Imani were now covering their heads and running in retreat. Chunks of ceiling fell as they were blown apart by the explosions. Everything around Uko and Imani was engulfed in the raging fire. The two of them flashed and flickered but neither was hurt at all by the chaos around them. Both of their eyes lit up with reflections of the magnificent destruction as the explosions continued. Reapers and Coyotes dashed in different directions to escape while a forcefield of calm surrounded Uko and Imani.

"I know where he is," Imani said suddenly. Even though she did not yell, he could hear her voice over the explosions and sounds of Reapers screaming as their cloaks caught fire.

"Your brother?" Uko asked and he turned away from the sight of everything around them. As he looked away from another explosion that claimed a group of fleeing Coyotes, he saw a streak of color that caught his attention. A royal blue that stood out in a room of black and gray cloaks and red fire entered his vision for a moment. He turned back to see where it came from and saw Chief staring back at him.

They locked eyes before Chief began to stalk toward Uko and Imani. Chief stepped over fallen Coyotes and burning Reapers without breaking his stride or his gaze. The intense firelight colored his black sunglasses as he walked. His blue dashiki and colorful scarves billowed but were never caught in the flames around him.

Uko opened his mouth to speak but couldn't. He was frozen in fear. As Chief closed the distance between them he reached out his hand. Uko looked down at the outstretched hand and saw a bright flash of light that nearly blinded him and forced him to shield his eyes with his arm. When he removed his arm and opened his eyes again, the fire, Imani, the Coyotes, Chief, and even the room were gone. Uko was no longer in the eye of a molten lava hurricane. He was in a park. With squirrels.

CHAPTER 13

Preteen Retirement

UKO STOOD ON A CONCRETE WALKWAY that was lined on both sides with weeping willow trees leaning over the path. Their branches crisscrossed each other and looked like the trees were holding hands to provide shade to the people below. Along the outside of the walkway were benches where people sat, read, played with children, and watched those who walked by. Uko was stunned by how different this was from what he'd just gone through. There were no Coyotes, no Reapers, and no all-consuming fire. There were only a dozen people enjoying a beautiful summer afternoon without a care in the world.

Uko walked down the path to a large stone water fountain. It was an enormous marble fountain with water shooting several feet into the air before falling to a basin filled with lucky pennies. Toni sat on its rim with her hand in the water. Uko smiled as they made eye contact and she stood up.

"I'm hoping that smile means good news and you're not just a crazy person," she said. She tucked curls of hair behind her ear and smiled back.

"It's nice to see you too, Toni."

"Uko!" Toni shouted, "Did you find her brother?!"

"Nope. She figured out where he was herself." Uko was trying to keep up the cool guy vibe he found in the dream with Imani. It was nearly impossible with Toni. Everything inside him wanted to hug her, jump up and down, and scream like they'd won the lottery.

"Even better," Toni laughed as she patted Uko on the back. "I'm just messing with you. I knew you did it as soon as I saw your goofy face. You're in my dream because you did it, buddy," Toni said. "You're officially a Nightmare Detective. You made it!"

She stepped back to get a better view of Uko as he took in the news. She shook her head wordlessly side to side in a motion that meant no but with eyes that said yes. "I'm so happy," she finally said quietly to herself without moving her lips. Uko thought she may not have realized he heard her say it. He left it alone.

"We didn't go find her brother. She told me she knew where he was, but we never went to find him," Uko said.

"That's fine. It happens sometimes," Toni responded. "You just need to help them solve the mystery. Even if they don't go through with the final steps, as long as they know what to do, it's fine. What exactly happened after I left?"

"I almost gave up. It was the worst feeling ever," Uko replied. "But it got worse. The Skeleton King came."

"Makes sense," Toni said. "When you have your lowest moments, doubt creeps in. He lives off that. But obviously you didn't let it stop you."

"I guess," Uko said. "Imani turned around after everything seemed hopeless. You remember how helpful and nice she was when you were there?" he asked laughing a bit at the memory.

"She was clearly jealous," Toni replied. They both laughed at the thought.

After calming down and wiping a tear from his eye, Uko continued. "We got captured by Coyotes and she got us out by pretty much making the room explode around us. It was crazy."

"Speaking of which," Toni said as her tone shifted. "I'm a little worried about Coyotes following us into that nightmare. I don't know what you did to get on their radar, but this is strange. First you meet Chief and now you're trying to pass your Detective test while Coyotes are going all out to stop you."

"Chief was in the nightmare."

"What?"

"He was there. At the end. I heard him yell when Imani figured everything out. And then when the room came crashing down, he came after me. I was so scared I was stuck. But before he got to me, everything flashed like someone was taking a picture and I ended up here."

Toni stared at Uko in shocked silence.

"I guess he didn't like me telling him no in my dream and he came to make me fail my test," Uko said. "That didn't turn out well for him."

Toni smiled and sat back down on the edge of the fountain. "I guess so. You got saved by the bell. Once she figured it out and you passed, you were pulled here. Great." She dipped her hand into the water and stared at the ripples. "This is my favorite park in Savannah. My family and I try to come here every weekend if the weather's nice."

Uko sat at the fountain next to her. "What happens to us now?"

"Now I move on. I retire," Toni said. "You replace me as a Nightmare Detective and carry on the legacy. Hopefully, you help hundreds and hundreds of kids and when it's finally your turn to call it quits, you find someone even more amazing than yourself."

"What if I just stay with you? I'd rather do that than be a Detective," Uko said, surprising himself. Cool guy mode was officially off the table now.

Toni looked up from the fountain to Uko. The pursed her lips and shook her head.

"I'm serious," Uko said.

"You can't stay with me. You're a Detective. That's your mission now," Toni replied. She looked back to the fountain and signed. "You've got more important things to take care of."

"No, I don't," Uko said.

Toni looked back at Uko with a pained smile. "I know you feel that way now. But you'll grow out of it. And you'll end up as one of the greatest Detectives of all time," she said.

Uko looked down at his folded hands in his lap. He got the point. "Can we at least keep in contact?"

"In Pangea?"

"No, real life."

Toni didn't say anything for a few seconds. "I don't know if that would be a good idea. Don't know of many retired detectives who keep in contact with their mentees in real life."

"There's a first time for everything."

Toni chuckled and stood up. "Look at you. All clever and whatnot now?"

Uko blushed.

"You have to focus on being a Detective," Toni said. "What you'll be doing is important. You're building kids up, so they can deal with the world when it tries to break them down."

Uko opened his mouth to protest. Toni raised a hand to stop him. When he did, she continued softly, "When I recruited you to join, we were constantly fighting the Skeleton King. I helped you learn how to defeat him, even if you don't remember the other nightmares we were in together. Each one built you up a little. Other people need that help. Everybody has their own Skeleton King," Toni said. "Now," she said in an exaggeratedly excited tone, "tell me more about what you did to save your little girlfriend, Imani."

"I don't wanna to talk about myself," Uko said, feeling more deflated than he ever have.

"Fine. I'll just make up the details in my head," she said. They both looked at the fountain in silence while kids played around them.

"Well, as far as going into dreams on your own, you'll be using the DreamHub that we used before. That hub will be what connects you to everyone else in Pangea. It lets you see glimpses of things going on to people all over the world as they dream."

Uko looked at her with an annoyed look on his face. This conversation wasn't going the way he thought it would. The last thing he wanted to talk about was being a Detective. Toni ignored his expression and continued.

"In the beginning it's hard to make out what you see, but you'll get the hang of it eventually. Just concentrate on the images. When you enter a nightmare, you'll notice that the image you saw in the DreamHub was sort of like a preview of things. When we went into the nightmare with the crayon dinosaurs, I remember the DreamHub image we chose kinda looked like a dinosaur."

Uko sighed loudly and looked to the sky. He had to accept that this was would be the way would be. Better that than to spend their last few moments upset. "So, I fall asleep, I walk through the Silk Road, get to the Dreamhub, and I pick one to enter," Uko asked.

"Pretty much," Toni replied. "It's really cool when you start doing it. I would spend my whole life staring at the Dreamhub and jumping around Pangea if I could. Much better than school."

"Yeah I can see that."

"How's the Griot's notebook been going?"

Uko had difficulty continuing. He wanted to leave now that he'd been rejected, but he knew he'd come to regret that decision. He took a deep breath and raised his head. "I love it. It's filled with so many different stories about people's lives in Pangea that I feel like I've been here forever," he said. He did love the book, he just wished he could talk about it under different circumstances. "I wish

I had the other volumes. I've read mine cover to cover already."

"You should spend the rest of the summer hunting down the other versions."

"I think I will," Uko said. The thought had already crossed his mind multiple times.

Toni stood up and began to walk down the path Uko traveled to meet her at the fountain. She motioned for him to join him. When he caught up to her, she had a huge vanilla ice cream cone covered with chocolate sprinkles in her hand. She grinned before licking.

"How did you—"

"I'm very good at my job."

Uko laughed. "How do I get as good as you?"

"You mean how do you get better," Toni said with sprinkles on her nose.

"You're right. How do I get better," Uko said as he brushed the sprinkles off.

"Take it seriously. You already have the gift. Now, you just need to keep working on it. Remember that every dream or nightmare leaves clues that you need to notice. Some are small, and others are obvious but the more you pick up on, the more helpful you'll be. You gotta be Sherlock Holmes when you step into Pangea," Toni said. "It's important. It's a calling. When you come to work every night, you're helping someone build reality."

"If it's so important, we should do it for everyone—not just kids," Uko said. "We should do it for as long as we can, so we keep getting better and better. We should fight against the people, like the Coyotes, who are doing the opposite of what we're trying to do."

He expected Toni to repeat the rules to him; to remind him that it's dangerous to live in nightmares for too long and remind him that they can only help so many people so why not focus on those who are open to the lessons. Instead she just smiled and licked her ice cream.

"That's why I like you," she said. "You're gonna be great at your job. The real world and Pangea are both filled with people like the Coyotes. Maybe you'll help make them both a little better."

Uko blushed again. "If it wasn't against the unwritten Detectives rules, would you want to stay in contact with me?"

Toni paused. "Yes," she said quietly.

"What's your last name?" Uko asked.

"Why?"

"No reason," Uko lied.

"You plan on looking me up?"

"Yup."

Toni blushed. "Can't make it that easy, can I? You're a Detective now. Crack the case."

Uko felt the same electrical surge he felt in Imani's nightmare. Uko held up her half-eaten ice cream cone to him. "Let's just enjoy this last dream together in my favorite park. Have some ice cream."

Uko looked at her over the ice cream between them before taking a lick.

"The ice cream tastes good, right?" Toni asked.

"I normally hate chocolate. Hate it. But this is different," Uko responded. The ice cream tasted like victory. "This has to be the best ice cream I've ever had."

Toni smiled. "Amen to that."

CHAPTER 14

Be Careful with Me

UKO WOKE UP TO THE QUIET stillness of his bedroom. He looked around and thought about the hectic final test he finished before saying goodbye to Toni. He was finally a Nightmare Detective. His mixed feelings of becoming what he wanted so badly while losing Toni were hard to process. He told himself that his mission would be to find her in the sleep walking world, no matter how long that took.

After lying in his bed for a few minutes, Uko reached under it to pull out the Griot notebook. Whenever he wanted to daydream about the Pangean world, he read the stories of its inhabitants. He flipped through the pages slowly, looking for an entry he hadn't read recently.

The pages were well worn from the notebook's age and being poured over ten to twenty times each. Toward the back he noticed, for the first time, the corner of one of the pages bent slightly. When he tried to straighten out the bend, he noticed the page was slightly thicker than the others in the notebook. He grabbed the bend again and peeled it down carefully, revealing a hidden page behind it. After a few moments of careful work, he separated the two pages that were previously stuck together without tearing the pages. Excited, he began reading the only entry in the notebook he never saw before.

Clement Hughes   March 31, 1996   9:13 AM

The only reason I'm doing this is to set the record straight. My reputation is not a trivial thing. I've done more to rise to where I sit today than most can imagine. But, for some reason, I don't get the respect that is owed to me. Don't they know I've slept on the Isle of the Dead for sport? How can I fear death in Pangea if I've vacationed in the destination of the damned?

They've heard of the horrors of Shaka the Butcher and her rage. They've warned their friends of Hannibal. They've seen entire armies built to protect civilians from Ras. Yet, they don't respect the only man able to tame these animals. The accomplishments of a wartime leader are never enough.

I'm used to this. Being able to see over the horizon has been what's kept me here. I know at some point there will be someone who challenges me with the support of other Pangeans. I want you to report this so those people don't doom themselves to misery. Don't find yourself trying to be a hero because heroes die uncomfortable deaths. Shaka and Ras live for conflict. I am conflict. There's a reason they are Coyotes and I am their leader. They worship me. I'm their everything.

I am their Chief.

Uko stared at the final sentence in disbelief. After a full minute of his mind racing, he reread the entry. It was exactly what he thought it was. The Griot sat with Chief himself and Uko, of all people, held the record of it in his hand. Uko closed the notebook and stared at the wall. Slowly, he stood up, walked to his dresser, and picked up his cell phone. He sent a single group text before he sat back down on his bed.

"Four in the park...my house...ASAP!"

The duties of a wartime hero awaited.

THE END

ABOUT THE AUTHOR

Monk is a husband and father of two from Newark, NJ who enjoys creating adventures that represent the neighborhoods he grew up in. He performed in TV, film, and theater as an actor in NY before earning his MBA from Rutgers University. To read Monk's blog, see what he's working on now, and to get more stories from the world of Pangea, visit

www.monkinyang.com